SIMON PETRIE

WAYFARING STRANGER

First published in Australia in 2024

Please direct all enquiries to the publisher at:
fomalhaut451@gmail.com

ISBN 978-0-6483836-7-3

Typeset in Adobe Garamond Pro / Candara
Cover illustration by James Morrison

National Library of Australia Cataloguing-in-Publication entry

Title: Wayfaring Stranger / Simon Petrie.
ISBN: 9780648383673 (pbk.)
Subjects: Science fiction, Australian.
Other Authors / Contributors:
               Morrison, James, editor.
               Morrison, James, cover art.
Dewey Number: A823.4

SIMON PETRIE

WAYFARING STRANGER

also by simon petrie

(the titan sequence)

Matters Arising from the Identification of the Body

Wide Brown Land

Soft Dim Skies

Flight 404

Murder on the Zenith Express: the Gordon Mamon collection

80,000 Totally Secure Passwords That No Hacker Would Ever Guess

Tremendously Inconveniencing A Great Many Photons

The 1001 Top Immortality Treatments You Must Try Before You Die

For T and D

who quite fell for each other

a frontloaded infodump
or, if you will,
a foreword

Those of you who've read my Titan stories might be a little surprised to learn that Saturn's smog moon isn't really my personal favourite among the settings I've explored within my science fiction. After all, there are three of my books set there, a number I intend to add to; my Titan fiction comprises a substantially larger number of stories, and of words, than I've devoted to anywhere else.

The 'anywhere else' which most captivates my imagination is a world which, up until now, has featured only in two of my early hard-SF stories: 'Downdraft', first published in *Sybil's Garage* issue 6, and 'Talking with Taniwha', which first appeared in *Borderlands* issue 11, both in 2009, a year before my first Titan story saw the light of day.

It isn't obvious, either, that 'Downdraft' and 'Talking with Taniwha' are connected; and aside from setting, they're not. Neither story impacts upon the other; they don't even share the same epoch. The place, the world, which provides their only sense of connection is a planet which, for no especially good reason, I have called Rousseau.

You might well wonder, if I'm saying it's my favourite setting, why I've written so few stories set on Rousseau, and so many on Titan. The answer is that, compared to Titan, we really don't know much about Rousseau, and lack of knowledge is problematic in the writing of hard SF. The reason *why* we know so little about Rousseau is that it doesn't exist. There's still no irrefutable evidence of worlds of this type within our

Galaxy, and no particularly good reason to expect that they would be inhabited. And yet…

Let me tell you a story. A *true* story, so far as we know.

A bit over four-and-a-half billion years ago, the protosolar nebula was busy going about its necessary business of condensing, accreting, and partitioning material into something that would ultimately be dubbed the Sun, surrounded by a then still rather unruly assembly of things that would eventually be called planetary bodies moving on trajectories that could in due course be termed orbits. The protosun grew warm, then hot, fed initially by the heat of gravitational contraction and then by the burgeoning fire of nuclear fusion, until it began to shine, and there was an end to the unending night.

Whatever form that first dawn took, it provoked change: anything volatile within the inner system was efficiently swept outwards, and in many cases clean away, by evaporation, sublimation, and the solar wind. What remained was a chaotic dodgem-car whirl of rubble from which almost all volatile material had been lost. I view it as being like the asteroid belt, but pervasively so throughout the inner system, and crowded with objects which hadn't yet had the time to learn to be orbitally nice to each other. Order was slowly established through a myriad collisions, which in many cases—*thanks, gravity*—wrought growth. Ultimately, this process yielded what we now know as the Solar System's inner ('terrestrial') planets: Mercury, Venus, Earth (and its Moon, stepdaughter of ill-fated Theia) and Mars. Fast forward, if you wish, to the present day.

Remember how I said the volatile material had been lost from the rubble from which the terrestrial planets formed? This means that these building blocks, these protoplanets (and, by extension, these subsequent planets) were composed of material which chemists would categorise as 'refractory': metal and rock.

Metal is its own thing, and scarcely requires definition (although, somehow, astrophysicists mean something different by the word than do chemists and all sensible people; I'm using it here in the objectively correct chemical sense, of elements that, in their pure form, are somewhat profligate with their electrons and are therefore generally good at conducting electricity). Rock is also undeniably its own thing, but is not (in a chemical sense) elemental, and therefore merits further categorisation. Rock, to a first approximation, can be thought of as metal oxide: *i.e.*, the chemical combination of metals with oxygen. And it's true that, ignoring the thin film of biosphere on Earth, the tenuous swathe of atmosphere on Mars, and the more substantial but still planetarily negligible atmospheric cloak of Venus, the inner 'terrestrial' planets can very reliably be regarded as rocky bodies with a denser metallic core. That, after all, is what metal, plus rock, plus gravity, plus sufficient warmth, will net you.

But this outcome is not inevitable. Let's dig a little deeper, to understand why.

When a protosolar nebula forms (or when, more generally speaking, a proto*stellar* nebula forms, because the Sun is but a star), it does so by a process of gravitational collapse within an already somewhat dense expanse of space; within what is known as a *dense interstellar cloud* or, alternatively, as a *dark cloud* or *molecular cloud* or, for the most expansive and most prolifically star-forming such objects, sometimes as a *giant molecular cloud*, all of which are, as is the wont of astrophysicists, reasonably prosaic and fairly accurately descriptive names, though one could quibble at the use of the word 'dense' to describe a volume of space several orders of magnitude less concentrated with gas than is, for example, the 'vacuum' at which the International Space Station orbits the Earth. But let us not dwell overmuch on the vagaries of well-intended terminology…

I've been fascinated by dense interstellar clouds for about four decades now, because they combine two of my very favourite things: space and chemistry. Dense interstellar clouds are the places where nearly new and ages-old atoms alike first form molecules, fed by the cold, the lack of disruptive light, and the comparatively high probability of one drifting atom meeting another drifting atom on a better-than-daily basis. The molecules they form are to some degree dictated by the relative abundances of their precursor atoms, though the intrinsic stability of a molecule is also important, of course, as an influence on its longevity. It's not too surprising to learn that by far the most abundant molecule in a typical dense interstellar cloud is hydrogen, H_2, since the hydrogen atom vastly outnumbers all other heavier atoms. The second most abundant molecule, carbon monoxide (CO), is formed from two of the most abundant of those heavier-than-hydrogen singletons.

Both H_2 and CO are very volatile; they prefer to exist as gases, and only condense out under what we'd mark as extreme cold. Let's store that fact away for later, because there's something rather special about carbon monoxide, aside from its abundance within the universe, and its volatility, and here's where this story gets interesting.

Carbon monoxide has the strongest bond from carbon to any other atom. It has the strongest bond from oxygen to any other atom. It has, in fact, so far as we know, the strongest chemical bond of any in existence, at least among molecules at all likely to arise without artificial intervention. What this means is that, once carbon monoxide forms, in the depths of a dense interstellar cloud, it doesn't really want to change into another molecule through chemical reaction. What it also means is that any lone carbon atom in such a cloud is really, really, really keen to meet a nice oxygen atom to form CO with, and, analogously, any single oxygen atom of good breeding must be in want of a carbon atom with which to settle down, if only it can find one. But life isn't always fair, and dense interstellar clouds generally aren't perfectly balanced in terms of their oxygen and carbon content. Some will have more carbon than oxygen (C/O > 1) and some more oxygen than carbon (C/O < 1). What happens to the surplus atoms, that can't form CO?

In 'oxygen-rich' interstellar clouds, they form water, with hydrogen; and rock, with available metal atoms.

The Sun, and its retinue of planets (including the Earth), formed from a protosolar nebula that originated within an oxygen-rich dense interstellar cloud. Consequently, when the Sun blew away the water and other volatiles from the inner solar system and left the refractory material more-or-less intact, that planet-forming refractory material was metal and rock, as noted above. But what if the protostellar nebula happened to have been within a carbon-rich interstellar cloud, a class of object known to occur quite widely within the Galaxy?

In 'carbon-rich' interstellar clouds, the carbon atoms efficiently consume the available oxygen to form carbon monoxide, but that can still leave quite a bit of carbon for which CO formation isn't an option. Oxygen forms the strongest bond to carbon, but other bonds are possible when oxygen is no longer available, so these 'surplus' carbon atoms form organics (which are somewhat volatile at sensible temperatures) and 'network solids' such as diamond and carbides (which aren't) from whatever other material remains to hand.

In a C-rich protostellar nebula, waiting for that first dawn of nuclear fire within its protostar, the inner-system volatiles are mainly CO and organics, and the planet-forming refractories are metal, carbides… and diamond. Potentially, quite a lot of diamond.

Potentially, enough diamond to form a very thick diamond mantle around a denser metallic core, in just the same way as Earth has a thick silicate and rock mantle surrounding a denser metallic core.

'Diamond planets' (I myself prefer the label 'carbonaceous planets') almost certainly exist within our Galaxy, because the carbon-rich dense interstellar clouds from which they would naturally arise definitely do exist. We can't straightforwardly identify such planets, because determining the geologic composition of small non-luminous bodies at astronomical distances is still, one might say, a black art… but they're out there, somewhere.

Of course, Venus, Earth, and Mars are not merely rocky bodies. There's that atmospheric skin, and in Earth's case a hydrosphere and a curious panoply of living things. Whether, in our Earth's case, this non-rocky material was retained against the odds during planetary formation, or gained through subsequent accretion (cometary impacts and the like) is still a topic of debate. But it's notable that the atmospheres of Venus, Earth, and Mars are all oxidising atmospheres… the kind of atmosphere one might naturally expect to arise through the weathering of rock.

What kind of atmosphere might we expect to persist (or to arise through weathering) on a carbon-rich planet?

An organic one. Just as we'd suspect any bodies of surface liquid to be organic (i.e. carbon-rich), rather than the hydrogenated oxygen in which Earth's fish swim.

Now, we don't have any organic-dominated environments in the inner solar system. We do, though, in the outer solar system (that is, in the region of the Sun's domain within which its ability to sweep space clear of volatiles could best be described as 'faltering'). One such object— and here I loop back to my favourite Solar System world, Titan—gives us a quite useful indication of the properties of an organic-dominated atmosphere, and of the planetary characteristics of surface liquid organics.

Are there any grounds to expect that a carbon-rich planet might be capable of producing and sustaining life? We probably can't answer that reliably just yet. We can presume that Titan itself is probably too cold to be life-bearing, whatever the prospects might be for its colonisation. But biochemistry is versatile, and life on Earth has experience with several substantially different pathways towards the harnessing of materials and energy on which living matter depends…

Suppose it *were* possible for life to exist on a diamond-mantled, organic-crusted planet, perhaps one larger and substantially warmer than Titan itself… what might this life be like?

Wayfaring Stranger is an attempt at an answer to that question, as well as an adventure in its own right. I hope you enjoy the speculation.

Simon Petrie
November 2024

one

She'll remember this conversation weeks later, as she falls. But by then, it will be much too late.

Daycycle 41, mid-shift 1/ WS-352.32R

She's talking with Liam, over coffee, in the airship's rec lounge.

Liam is moderately tall. Awkwardly thin. Thick fuzz of copper hair, weak watery eyes, bulbous nose. Liam's most prominent feature, though, is an Adam's apple that juts so confrontingly Solveig expends much time, and not a little discomfort, in monitoring it while it bobs. She's half-afraid it's going to breach the skin at some point. She's not even looking at it: she's straining to meet his eyes, though he's more than a head taller. Yet she can't help but be absorbed by the Adam's apple, its sliding rhythm of light and shade, ascending, descending, through her peripheral vision.

It'd be a pity, she decides, if she stayed fixated on Liam's thyroid. It turns out he's got some interesting things to say. She's feeling slightly embarrassed at having discounted him, earlier, on the grounds that he's Trade, not Science. Add it to the tally beside the throat-lump thing, throw in the unease that still comes, occasionally, with sixteen kilometres' worth of altitudinal awareness: she's not at her most relaxed.

Liam, though, Liam, he's entirely comfortable, and she envies that; she'd wish to borrow some of that, if she could. Check out some confidence, a decent supply of self-assurance. Perhaps also an allotment of equanimity from the *Wayfaring Stranger*'s store, indefinite loan, return when no longer required. Something like that.

Now he waves his arm, casual as what-you-please, towards the viewport with its display of the sky; with its coloration that still gives her trouble. The sky shades to haze towards the horizon and below. The airship's shadow, a distended, amorphous smudge, stretches across the upper reaches of the sepia-clotted haze-deck a few kilometres beneath them. A large flock of viridescent bloons drifts towards the top corner of the viewport, harried by a silver-bright ribbonwing, up where the sky is bluer, blindingly bright. She keeps having to remind herself that Rousseau can indeed *do* bright: down below, on the haze-shrouded planet's twilit-at-best surface, you'd never believe it. (As it is, the *Wayfaring Stranger* is not truly atop all of the atmosphere's haze, though aside from the lingering hours of sunrise and sunset, the skeiny, diffuse layers of it stacked several kilometres above the airship are distinctly more difficult to discern than is the thick and nearly opaque brown-black carpet of the lowest haze-deck.)

Elsewhere, and much further out than the bloons, she can spy a smattering of bubbleheads. There are also a few faraway wisps of faux smoke churned up from the haze-deck by currents, or by the passage of some large aerial creature. The almost-regular meshwork of a half-grown doily, its rippling crosshatched framework studded by gummy knots of toxin, accompanies the tentative tendrils of updrifted haze, blindly seeking contact with whatever prey it might encounter. Solveig sees, too, what looks like a dangler, its lethal tentacles trailing from a shiny translucent envelope. Behind the bloons, indistinct through distance and dust yet so obviously large that, at several kilometres, it can scarcely be anything else, *looms a zep...*

Liam has said something just now. Solveig didn't hear it, zoned out as she was on the rec lounge's panoramic view. This is something that's been happening quite a bit. (Plus, lately, the Adam's apple.) She waits, hoping he'll provide context for what she's missed.

He adds, 'But they don't *have* to make sense, do they? At least, not to us. I mean, they're alien.'

She redirects her full attention back to him, is fairly sure he hasn't even been looking at the viewport, so accustomed is he to the wonders of Rousseau's upper atmosphere, its 'clean air'. Because, well, he's seen it, hasn't he? Fifteen months on the *Wayfaring Stranger* so far, he'd said. She's envious, and a little unsettled, at the familiarity with this environment that such a duration implies. Fifteen months, continuously, never descending below the haze deck. Fifteen months of disorienting protracted days, fifteen months of age-long nights lit by the bloons' golden phosphorescence, fifteen months sighting needlehawks, lancegliders, floatcarpets, mantawings... She wonders if she'll be so inured, so blasé, after fifteen months. That's if the admins allow her anywhere *near* that duration up here.

'No, I disagree,' she says, after a thoughtful sip at her cooling black coffee. 'Just because they're alien, it doesn't excuse them from the laws of the universe. Things like nutrition, reproduction, mortality, they all operate in fundamentally the same fashion, for all that they look superficially very different here on Rousseau than they would on Earth.'

'Oh, I know *that*,' he explains, and this time he does turn his attention to the view. 'That wasn't the kind of sense I was talking about.' He points. 'I meant, okay, tell me what that zep's thinking?'

Solveig's impressed that he's already perceived it, without ostensibly window-gazing in the way she can't currently help doing. 'He's probably wondering why we're tailing—'

'She.'

'How can you tell? From this distance?' (Unspoken: *And you, a mere tech, not a xenist*. But doesn't this make her no better than the rest?)

'Never see the males down this low. But my point is, okay, their ways of being presumably make sense, some way or other, but we don't know—'

'We know they're sentient. We learnt that from the taniwha, and we've surmised as much from a few distant vocalisations. The hexadecimal thing, and all that. We'll... progress beyond that at some point.'

With something better than interspecies hearsay and some unfathomable eavesdropped dialogue.

'Will we, though? It's been thirty years. I would've thought—'

'I've had some experience in conversing with aliens,' she says, casting her mind back to the taniwha, on what feels like a different world. 'It can seem as though there are long patches of unproductive floundering and hopeless crosstalk. But often, you're making progress even when it doesn't feel like it. As are they, for that matter.'

'That's assuming both sides are happy to talk,' he answers, flicking a meaningful glance in the distant zep's direction. 'It's a fair bet that one's not moving towards us.'

Solveig follows his gaze, and nods ruefully. She's going to run out of coffee soon, and with it the pretext for prolonging this conversation. 'Well ... no. I suspect you're right. What's the closest they've ever let the *Stranger* approach?'

'About that. You'd think, the envelope shape and all that, they might be more accepting of an airship, but they'll actually let— ah, but you'll know all that.'

'I'm not exactly a zep expert, Liam. Pond life's been more my thing, before this.'

'Things are looking up for you, then.'

'Maybe. Hope so. But why is that, d'you reckon, that they don't let the airship close? Do you think it's a size thing, or what?'

'Hell, who knows? Could just be that we're blocking their view. But you're the xenopsychologist, you tell me.'

'Linguist.'

'Same thing,' Liam replies, grinning.

The airship shifts a little, a tilt and a dip, as a wind gust pushes against it: a reminder, she thinks, not to get too comfortable, too complacent. She keeps her footing with a difficulty he doesn't seem to share. *We don't belong here, in this air.* A few seconds later, the bloons scatter and regroup in the wake of the same disturbance. 'You want another coffee?' she asks.

'No, better get back to it. Good talking to you, though, Doc.'

'Solveig,' she corrects.

'Got it.' He accepts her empty cup, places it with his on the mag-clamped trolley by the door, and moves off towards, she presumes, the plant room.

He's got a nice walk, she decides, and wonders if it's disloyalty, or something other, to think that he looks better from behind than from the front.

Hopefully it isn't disloyalty, because she's concluded that she rather likes Liam. As a coffee companion, if nothing else. There's been something ... *refreshing* about their dialogue. To talk things over with a non-scientist: no sense of turf wars, no point-scoring, no vindictive, combative, vituperative petty squabbling. None of the usual mutual defensiveness, the sense of competition that comes with too few fieldwork slots. *He's talking because he's interested, and maybe even because he hopes to learn something. Not because he hopes to invalidate, or to influence, or to see if I've got anything he can misappropriate* ... She's surprised, now, at the strength of her feeling, wonders whether it's the coffee that has her riled up, or that she genuinely feels such a depth of animosity towards Jens, and Herrick, and Xiaomei.

Jens, perhaps, she decides. Not the others, though they could have stood up for her. But Jens actively screwed her over.

She turns, for another look out that captivating viewport, and is bemused to note that one of the *Wayfaring Stranger*'s several fearless maintenance drones is suckering its way across the viewport's outer surface, scraping off what it can of the sepia-toned coating of organics that has built up over the past few days. There's now a strip, a fairly broad though imperfectly marked vertical stripe, from which the accumulated crud has been abraded free, and the contrast between the two zones is quite dramatic. It's not just that the view through the cleaned portion of the viewport is brighter, though of course that plays a part; it's that the 'blue' seen through the coated portion can now plainly be seen to be counterfeit, a shade of murky green that the eye tricks the brain into *believing* to be blue, because that is the expected colour.

The drone slips, and for a moment she is convinced that it is going to fall. But it remains attached in some manner, repositions itself, and continues to go about its task as though the sixteen-kilometre gulf beneath it is of no consequence.

two

Daycycle 42, shift 1 / WS-352.56R

The *Wayfaring Stranger*'s labspace, on the gondola's middle deck, lacks any of the viewing areas that the gondola's few public recreational zones—the rec lounge, the self-serve, the games room—possess. Consequently, there are no distracting views, unless you count the chamber's warning-emblazoned escape port, stocked with skysuits, helmets, parachutes.

Xeno-research is characterised by the necessity to work—indeed, to live—within a strictly confined volume. The labspace, though well-equipped to Solveig's somewhat nonexpert eye, would struggle to accommodate, at any one time, more than four of the six researchers who share its resources; fortunately, it seldom needs to. Fortunately, also, Solveig's own preferred workbench—by reason of its distance from the instrumentation consoles and biocontainment booths—is also the least preferred working surface of her more apparatus-dependent colleagues, and is therefore generally available even when the more highly sought sectors of the room's research real estate have been claimed. Up until the previous daycycle's zep sighting, her workspace has been entirely adequate. It's never been tidy, exactly: her personal setting for 'order' is not the same as, say, Torsten's. Now, though, what remains of the visible surface of her bench space is a chaos of tools, note-pods, and miscellaneous components. That said, there's not much visible surface, thanks to the featherweed.

The featherweed's a fake, an artificial construct designed to carry a sufficiently-large hydrogen bladder for buoyancy and an array of small long-life propulsion units for mobility and attitude control. Its payload is a set of surveillance lenses, mics, and a transmitter. It's intended to resemble a specimen of aeroflora known to have a biochemistry sufficiently weaponised as to render it unpalatable to much of the animal life found in Rousseau's upper atmosphere. It is, therefore, a perfect design for close-up observation of a zep.

At least, it *should* be a perfect design for this purpose, once she gets it correctly functioning. Again.

Elsewhere around the labspace's wall-facing workstations, Rewi is printing off a batch of filters for his microbiome sampling rig; Bao is working the controls of their containment chamber. Within the containment chamber's triply glazed panelling, some hapless specimen of aeroflora—a bubblehead this time, Solveig thinks—has been shepherded for perusal (read: inspection; read: analysis; read: destruction). Solveig has always been rather squeamish about the more ruthless aspects of xeno-research, the need for creatures to be killed in the pursuit of biological and biomolecular knowledge. At least Bao's field is botany, rather than zoology like Torsten's and Hong's, but it doesn't help that the plantforms are capable of a degree of independent motion.

Solveig returns her attention to the task at hand. She has interrogated each component on her featherweed three times this morning: individually, they're all performing to spec. But the featherweed isn't. And it's not providing any hints as to why that's so.

This, she thinks, planing her free hand across her brow, is the part of xenolinguistics she finds utterly dispiriting. Not the uncertainty over a nuance of translation, the agonising over the possibility of inadvertently causing offence, the pulling of evasive meaning out of an often impossibly tangled net of noise, gesture, and contextual clutter: that's what makes it worthwhile. That's where the achievement is. What she hates is when the equipment won't work.

The equipment is her Achilles' heel. The architecture of an alien brain she can, given time, make headway within; but, beyond a niggling suspicion that the featherweed doesn't 'look right', she's out of ideas.

She's not a tech, she's quite probably the least tech-minded of any of the scientists onboard, but sometimes it's necessary to pretend to be what you're not. (In her more cynical moods, she decides that this is pretty much the defining characteristic of intelligent life…) And this is one aspect of the culture aboard the *Wayfaring Stranger* to which she's had difficulty adjusting. At the lake station, where she was part of the team communicating with the taniwha population, there was a reasonably integrated cluster of scientists and technicians working in tandem. Here, so far as she's observed, that doesn't apply: there's a stratification, just like the gondola's division into decks. The scientists do science duties, the techs do tech duties, but they don't intermingle. Of course, an airship doesn't maintain itself to the extent that a lakeside habitat does, and there's the mass-premium argument, but still…

There are other ways, too, in which the attitude aboard the *Wayfaring Stranger* is different: there's less of an overweening concern about biocontainment. The biospheres of Earth and Rousseau are just too disparate for there to be much opportunity for cross-contamination. That is, she can observe all this with the crystal clarity of the still-fresh outsider; but she can't yet find her way into the swim of it. Her own groundhugger defaults, inculcated over more than a year on the haze-inflicted surface and aligned in any case with her natural caution, are at odds with the sense of … *relaxed acceptance* … that the *Wayfaring Stranger*'s longer-serving crew-members seem to have reached about their place on Rousseau. *Almost,* she thinks, *as though they know they belong here.*

But we don't belong here. We can never truly belong here.

We could take on the biosphere, Solveig thinks, *if we were feeling sufficiently crazy-brave. It's just the sort of hubristically entitled nonsense we'd come up with, if we're in-system long enough. If we become blind to the recognition of what a biological crime such an action would constitute. But we wouldn't win. Oxygen just can't find a purchase against so much hydrocarbon.*

She picks the featherweed up, awkwardly turns it over in her hands. It's not primed, not buoyed by hydrogen, but even so it's low-mass for such a large and rigid structure, more air-mattress than apparatus, and its centre of gravity always catches her off-guard. And even though it doesn't look right to her eyes, that's not the problem. Not all featherweeds look the same, and provided that the construct has enough about it to suggest 'featherweed' to the Rousseauvian aerofauna, they're likely to keep at a moderate distance from it. The actual problem is that the unit is now refusing to handshake with her node—and this is in the calm confines of the labspace, so heaven only knows what it'll be like once it's launched into the turbulent, chaotic, disorienting, heavily populated environment that is Rousseau's upper atmosphere—meaning that, however much data it might succeed in gathering, it doesn't at this stage look inclined to pass any her way.

'Either of you guys know how to get this unit handshaking again?' she asks, though she's not hopeful. 'It was greenlighting last night, but now it's playing uncooperative.'

'What's changed between then and now?' Bao asks, not looking up from the containment chamber's control strip. Bao is wiry, dark, possessed of a lilting contralto that, in other circumstances, might almost prove seductive—it remains a vocal tone which, even after two weeks aboard, Solveig still has considerable difficulty reconciling with its owner—and is almost invariably enveloped in a chemical haze of perfume so strong that it sometimes makes the eyes water.

'The *functionality*, B, weren't you listening?' Rewi says. Rewi is a generation older, slightly overweight, bald, and of such unusual pigmentation, somewhere the other side of lilac, that Solveig is sure he has derm-shaded at some point in his past, though she doesn't ask. 'You've re-initialised it, I'm presuming?' he continues.

'I've tried everything that's in the specs,' Solveig replies, allowing a degree of steel to enter her voice. She's faced with the twin handicap here: newcomer, and linguist—therefore, not a *proper* scientist—and she can feel the condescension in Rewi's tone every time he addresses her.

She shouldn't let it bother her, but she can't help it: she knows she's competent, capable, astute, adaptable—she's *talked with taniwha*, for fuck's sake, and if anyone can find a way to break through the zeps' resistance to communication with humans, it'll be—

(Does she dare to complete this thought?)

I have no room for arrogance, she tells herself, *when I can't even get the featherweed to communicate with my node. How dependent are my accomplishments…*

'I mean,' she perseveres, 'I can sig it from the node, it's got plenty of power, and the signal strength's good—'

'From two metres away, be something pretty bloody wrong if it wasn't,' Rewi notes, glancing up briefly then bending again to the business of slotting the filters along the hinged frame of the sampling rig.

'—but it's just flatlining in response. From two metres away, like you say.'

'Yeah, well,' says Bao, who doesn't seem to have looked up, all this time, from their own task which Solveig watches with a kind of squeamish fascination. It's ludicrous to think of the procedure as actually *cruel*, but it's disconcerting. (As Bao and Sanna have both explained to her, one of the peculiarities of lighter-than-air lifeforms is that conventional methods of dissection are of limited utility as a method of examination: with so much of the creature necessarily a reservoir for gases, and much of the metabolic freight carried by volatiles, there's a lot of information lost when one punctures a membrane. Which means that, before Bao's bubblehead can be microtomed, it must first be frozen; and frozen at such a rate—not too fast, not too slow—that its outer wall does not rupture or crack, and that as many of its internal partitions as possible remain intact down to liquid-nitrogen temperatures.) Already the bubblehead has a deflated and cloudy appearance. Bao finally makes eye contact with Solveig. 'That's not helpful at all,' they offer.

Not helpful at all, Solveig thinks acidly, *could describe a variety of things*. But this is uncharitable: the zep-comm project is hers alone, Rewi and Bao have their own research interests they're obligated to pursue, with which they don't expect her assistance or input; and in any case she has too great a tendency, she knows, to ascribe universal competence to those who don't necessarily possess it. Just because Rewi can print, pick clean, and analyse a Rouss-bac filter, and Bao can strip an airborne plant down to its main cellular constituents over a five-hour period, it does not follow that either of them know how to solve her problem: it's not *their* problem.

But it *is* a problem, and she cannot see how to solve it; she needs help. Help or coffee or … Liam.

Liam.

But, of course, there is no dead weight on an airship, and it's not as though Liam is simply waiting around to help out with whatever science glitches might have reared their heads. Liam is Trade, and kept well busy by the near-constant need for maintenance and vigilance in a toxic, crowded, and sometimes unpredictable aerial environment: aside from the more routine mechanical aspects of keeping an airship near-permanently aloft, there are the safety aspects that come with maintaining an oxygenated habitat suspended from a voluminous hydrogen envelope, as well as the security concerns posed by disguising said envelope as a zep and the crewed gondola as a severely oversized remora; for, while the zeps are sufficiently large and well-defended to have few active predators, there are creatures that hunt them, and there are others that prey on remoras. Thus, unusually for a research vessel, the *Wayfaring Stranger* is armed, although the preferred defensive measures are nonlethal.

She shouldn't be bothering Liam; but on the other hand, she's sure he's up with the play on this kind of thing: the maintenance drones, the cams, the microwave dissuaders, the anti-needlehawk turrets all need to communicate with the plant room ops, so it's a fair bet he knows the ins and outs of handshaking. It's likely that what's mountain to her will be merest molehill to Liam. And with this salve to her conscience, her mind's made up. She'll enlist Liam's help.

She looks up, almost expecting the others to have noticed something, but of course there's nothing for them *to* have noticed.

'Just going for coffee,' she announces, more for her own sake than anyone else's.

The grunt from Bao might be in response, or it might not.

Daycycle 42, shift 1 / WS-352.57R

Coffee is, indeed, an attractor, but the featherweed needs something that a caffeine jolt is unlikely to deliver, so she climbs up, not down, when she gets to the ladder.

It's mid-morning. The ladder, as well as the rest of the gondola, is shaded by the airship's envelope: zeps, and things that look like zeps, cast an extensive shadow, so there's a near-constant need for artificial lighting within all the quarters, even in full daylight. Outside, though, in the poisonous, busy air, Rousseau's sun is shining brightly on ribbonweed, on the ever-present bloons, and on something that looks like it might be frothswirl. Then she wonders if the *Stranger* has changed its heading completely over the past hour or so—which is possible, though she feels reasonably confident that she should have noticed—because she spies, at about the right distance but in completely the wrong direction, the zep…

But if it's the wrong *direction*, it's also the wrong *position*, because the sun hasn't shifted so much…

…or it's *not the same zep*. And at this thought, something catches fire within her, something that yearns to be out there among these creatures, just as, after a fashion, she had been 'out there' among the taniwha. Zep sightings are rare; zep gatherings have never been properly documented nor closely observed. This should be an opportunity for her to prove her mettle, but the featherweed—which would be her eyes and ears among these creatures—is currently lying, effectively dead, on her lab bench.

She allows her attention to linger on the new zep a few moments longer, as though concerned that such an emphatically substantial creature might somehow melt into the amber distance, before hauling herself out of the ladderwell.

At the entrance to the plant room, she's struck by a sudden rush of nerves. *Best just get it over with*, she tells herself, and pushes in. It surprises her, nonetheless, that though she genuinely doesn't belong in here, she somehow doesn't feel as out-of-place here as she does in the labspace, where she *does* (in principle) belong. It probably helps, nonetheless, that Liam's station is closest to the entrance. Less gauntlet to run.

'Sorry, you're busy,' she begins as he looks up.

'Just a little,' he replies, spreading his hands to indicate the displays of atmospheric containment status, envelope peripheral hazard monitoring, maintenance drone cam feeds, and… she's not actually sure what else. But at least he takes the time to smile, ever so slightly, as he says it. 'You've struck a problem, Doc?'

'Solveig,' she corrects. 'Look, I can come back at a better time—'

'I think now's as good a time as any,' he replies, and nods towards the plant room's other occupants, who seem to know to look up briefly at this juncture. 'Pretty sure Cordero and Isis can stop us all from plunging to our doom over the next few— how long is this problem of yours likely to take?'

'It's telemetry, so— not long, I think, but I really don't know. If I knew how long it would take to resolve, I'd probably know how to resolve it. But it's becoming urgent that I get the probe active. Liam, there's a *second zep* out there now.'

She doesn't expect the news to carry the same freight for him as it does for her: this almost-mystical, totemic significance, but the expression that catches on his face, as he turns to stare into her eyes, shows that he too is intrigued by this development. If not, perhaps, entirely surprised at the news: because he taps at the screen on his farthest right with a long index finger, turns to check it before turning back to her, and declares, 'Actually, no. There are three.'

Daycycle 42, intershift / WS-352.58R
When she gets back to the labspace with Liam—there's an almost palpable slap from the sharp topnote of Bao's perfume as they enter—

Rewi has absented himself, and Bao has taken advantage of their brief solitary occupancy of the labspace to fill the room not merely with scent, but also with song: a classical choral performance, female voices raised in a kind of pleasantly discordant harmony. *Music to deconstruct xenoflora by*, Solveig thinks, as she self-consciously leads Liam to her bench space. She glances at Bao—quite the day, this, for awkward glances—but the biochemist appears either oblivious to, or completely disinterested in, Liam's intrusion here. Not that this salves Solveig's conscience at having dragged him from his duties; nor her feeling of sheer vulnerability.

She's conscious, in contrast to his own ordered station, of just how messy her own bench is, with the featherweed squatting like a bad junior-school art project on her work-surface.

'This the probe you mentioned?' he asks.

She nods.

'May I?' he asks.

She nods.

He reaches out his left arm, his wrist brushing against her forearm in the process; she draws in a small breath, glances at Bao, but the other is still preoccupied in their analysis of the bubblehead's biomolecular componentry. *It's just a moment of accidental contact; it doesn't mean anything.*

Life is comprised of moments of accidental contact…

Liam has his hand on the featherweed, his head tilted to one side as though listening for something; he's diagnosing it, in much the same way as an old-school medical practitioner would once have used a stethoscope to ascertain ailments of the human frame. Solveig can only guess at the nature of the sensors he must have embedded in the palm of his hand.

'There's nothing wrong with its signalling ability,' he says after a half-minute or so.

'Which means the problem's internal, right?' Solveig asks.

'Reads that way, Doc.'

'Solveig,' she corrects, more or less on autopilot. Then adds, 'But it was sigging yesterday, and the only mods that have been made to it since then have been external. So how—'

'Beats me,' he replies. 'But that's the way it reads.'

'God, I'm sorry,' she says. 'I thought this was going to be something straightforward. I do feel really guilty about dragging you away from your work.'

'Well, don't,' he says, and lays a hand—an actual hand—on her shoulder, for a second or two, until he realises what he's done. 'Sorry,' he says. (But the gesture cannot be undone; nor does she think that she wants it to be.)

'But if it's internal, that could be almost anything—the circuitry, the comms ports, the—'

'Not having the probe blueprints to hand, there's still probably not that many things it could be. It has the *ability* to signal, it's just not doing so.'

'Jesus, it's just like a bloody zep,' she complains.

Bao looks up, this time, at his laughter.

'I'll bring up the plans for you,' she offers.

'Don't worry. I'll just have a rummage,' he announces, nudging the access port open. The featherweed's interior is, it seems to Solveig, an echo of the bench's messiness, a similar chaos with fewer elements, but Liam is not to be distracted by electronic disorder. Within a minute, it seems he's found what he's seeking. 'You make any adjustments to this since yesterday, when it was sigging?'

'Well, yes,' she concedes. 'But nothing that should impinge on its comms capability at all, according to the documentation. Just swapped out this faulty gyro for a supposedly-identical functioning module. Then I noticed that the new module was a gram or two heavier than the old one, which meant we weren't going to be at neutral buoyancy any more—I mean, we're not exactly talking sink-like-a-stone, but the thing wasn't going to float where we needed it to float—so I did a test inflation, a few more torr of hydrogen, and that didn't cause any mechanical issues. I purged it after that, so it was safe to work with, but it hasn't sigged since.'

'Soon have this sorted, Doc,' he says, and this time she doesn't 'Solveig' him. 'Pass me that reader?'

three

Daycycle 42, end of shift / WS-352.65R

Solveig would sooner avoid this—she finds the woman unsettling—but she can't allow the opportunity to dissipate.

She's accustomed to a certain commonality in the offices of senior academics: a desk; seating for both occupant and guests; shelves piled with data devices, mementoes and awards. Jens, she recalls, had within her office a guest-sensing display which, when activated, would present a never-quite-repeating 3-V testimonial highlighting achievements and encounters with notable personalities. Hong's alcove has nothing beyond the desk and two chairs. Solveig doesn't think such minimalism is weight-allowance-related, but she's not sure what is the intended message.

Hong, too, is similarly difficult to read: after inviting Solveig in, she doesn't even look up. Instead, she stays seated at her desk for several minutes, motionless. There's no work visible on the director's desk, but the seriousness of the pose quite emphatically warns against interruption. Perhaps she's communicating or organising, though her eyelids offer no hint of the REM-like saccades that would normally accompany such an activity, regardless of how deeply embedded she might be in conf mode.

The alcove is utterly still, save for the background thrum of the air-circulation system and the slight slow sideways slide of the airship's response to the subtly-shifting winds. Someone half a corridor-length away coughs. Solveig works at holding herself steady.

'Dr Robertson,' Hong says at length, in a fatigued don't-trifle-with-me voice, finally looking up at Solveig.

'Director,' replies Solveig. The wait has done nothing favourable to her resolve or her concentration. Perhaps that's the intent. 'I wish to stake a claim of priority.'

'In what resource?'

'Location.'

'On what grounds?' This, like the preceding question, is fired back quickly.

'Zeps,' Solveig says, mentally kicking herself. She's had an entire paragraph of argument running overnight through her head, emphasising the highly unusual circumstances and therefore importance of her claim, and all she can say is 'Zeps'. 'I mean—'

'I'm not mindful,' Director Hong responds. Pauses. 'To endorse your request.'

'Why?'

'Those aboard, and in more senior research positions than yourself, Doctor, have competing interests, have prior claims over our course that take priority. These claims are necessarily lodged substantially in advance and assessed by an expert panel comprising both science specialists and flight crew, so as to coordinate replenishment shipments as well as to set in place an ordered schedule for observational research. I need hardly explain that you, as the junior researcher amongst our ranks, cannot expect to be able to just drift in here on a whim and insist on some spur-of-the-moment—'

'It's hardly a whim.'

'But that's the effect. Now, if you will—'

'You haven't even asked me what my claim is.'

'I don't need to. In three R we need to be in position to commence the North of 50 programme. I'm not going to override that for the sake of a zep.'

'Not a zep,' Solveig argues. 'Zeps.'

'That doesn't change anything.'

'It should. Director, in the entire time we've been on Rousseau—so, fifteen years from first survey—there have been exactly two reported detections of zep congregation. Detection, not observation. We now appear to be ideally situated for close observation of a third such event—I mean, this will be the first time such observation would have been made. There are at least six zeps either in proximity to our current location, or inbound. I've checked the flight records; the Wayfaring Stranger has only ever passed within ten kilometres of an isolated zep on three occasions, and that's in over four years of service. We now have more zeps than that within that distance, simultaneously. I very strongly believe we should not allow that opportunity to go to waste.'

'There will be other chances. Even eclipses repeat, if you wait long enough. Bide your turn, Dr Robertson.'

'These are intelligent creatures. They've never shown any interest in initiating communication with us. They appear to have actively avoided us up until now. This behaviour now may signal a readiness on their part that hasn't been there before. I feel very strongly that we should not jeopardise that.'

'Conjecture.'

'No,' says Solveig, wondering at the lump that has formed in her throat. 'This is what I was taken on for.'

'You were taken on, Dr Robertson, as an adjunct researcher. A pair of hands. You'd do well to remember that.'

'I am more than a pair of hands, and you know it. This is an opportunity we have not had before, we may not have again. If we lose it, it will be remarked upon within the research community, whether you want it to be or not. It may not end up with only my reputation on the line over this.'

Hong fixes her gaze on Solveig. Stares. It's like being caught in a searchlight.

The searchlight blinks first.

*

Rousseau's biosphere is controlled by hydrogen, in somewhat the same way that Earth's is largely dominated by oxygen. It's not a direct correspondence, though. Hydrogen, on Rousseau, plays the role of lynchpin not principally for its chemical attributes (though there are some aeroforms, the needlesnouts and their kin, which do indeed consume it as a metabolite) but for its physical properties.

Take an atmosphere such as Rousseau's, predominantly nitrogen; some argon as always; but with a hefty proportion of various hydrocarbons. Provide a sun to illuminate said atmosphere with an abundance of visible and ultraviolet photons. Under such conditions, the inevitable products of photochemistry are an upper-atmospheric haze of larger and less volatile hydrocarbons, which will ultimately condense out; a complicated suite of nitrogen-containing organic molecules; and, if this junk is not rained out rapidly enough—and it often isn't—something that might as well be classed as 'soot' as anything else. All of which ensures that the planetary surface is shrouded in a perpetual oscillation between around fifty-eight hours of daylit half-darkness and as many of utterly black, starless night. Rousseau's thick, light-blocking haze deck is a forbidding impediment to any surface plant life, and by extension places a substantial limit on the types of niches that can be occupied by surface animal life.

But photochemistry giveth, just as photochemistry taketh away: for the photolysis of hydrocarbons can generate not merely haze, but also hydrogen. And hydrogen means buoyancy... if an organism can but produce it, or harvest it.

The planet's darkest and thickest haze layer cannot overshadow plants which succeed in floating atop it. This principle is the (literal) overriding characteristic of Rousseauvian life; but, baldly stated, thinks Solveig, it hints at little of the complexity and none of the beauty of Rousseau's lifeforms, whether that beauty be the almost dazzlingly silvered surfaces of the largest, highest-floating bloons; the deadly rococo messiness, like a minor composer's scrawled signature, drifting in the wake of a dangler's flamboyant envelope; the ponderous, aloof grandeur of the distantly looming zeps; or, though they are a sight seldom seen within the upper atmosphere (for they prefer, and are indeed better adapted to, the half-light beneath the haze), the rich fluoro-painted garishness of the montgolfiers...

Solveig releases the featherweed into an early afternoon sky during what, for her, is mid-morning, having once again cross-checked the camouflaged obs platform's vitals. She half expects it to plummet ruinously groundwards, or to glitch into unresponsive torpor; but it behaves as it should. Monitoring it from her now-almost-cleared workbench in the lab, she keeps it close by the gondola for several minutes, scudding it this way and that within the envelope's barely-slanted pillar of shadow, familiarising herself with the device's wristbanded controls, cascading through the various telemetry channels, until she dares to convince herself that the apparatus' continued operation is not just a transient fluke of good fortune. Then she pushes it out, into the sunshine of the wider sky.

She watches the display in fascination. She can see the living sky through the rec lounge viewscreen, of course, or through her own cabin's porthole, or onscreen courtesy of an array of several scopes affixed to the *Wayfaring Stranger*'s envelope, but the views transmitted by the featherweed are different in character, somehow; it's like seeing the world anew. The less-obviously impressive varieties of aerobiota—the loosely-tangled knots of floatweed, for example; the diffuse billowing sprawls of skybramble with their skittering nimbuses of small insectoidal fliers, drawing the injudicious attention of larger creatures towards their hosts' lethal, quick-flinging, thorn-studded whips; the flocks of languidly turning translucent green gyres, still not reliably categorised between slow-moving animal and carnivorous plant—she now sees these entities through, somehow, more personal eyes, a more intimate, more interactive view. And in immanent sunlight, not anchored within shade, which probably accounts for some of the difference.

The smaller lifeforms are fascinating in their own multitudinous ways, but it's the zeps that hold Solveig in thrall. For all their bulk and their apparent lack of any method of propulsion they are, she thinks, remarkably graceful creatures, capably of rapidly changing their heading—if not their direction of drift—by the displacement of ballast liquid to various nodes of the attitude sinus enmeshed within each zep's animate crust, its shell of subdermal tissue surrounding the voluminous, partitioned central void of buoyancy gas. She watches as the zep now central to her field of view turns face-on, against the prevailing wind, using a smooth combination of 'roll' and 'pitch' manoeuvres to effect a 'yaw' motion that it can't manifest directly. It's a beautiful action to witness, when one understands the mechanism behind it, as counterintuitive and as elegant in its own way as the bizarre and inherently unstable kinematic construct that is the bipedal locomotion her own kind has mastered. She finds herself flushed with a wave of awe, at the zep and at the biosphere which has produced it.

Store this moment, she tells herself. *Store it away for when you need it. For when someone well-meaning asks you whether research doesn't just strip all of the joy out of nature. Because you need to remember that while science can diminish mystery, it can also enhance wonder.*

And tell this to Liam, she adds. Not because she has any sense that he genuinely needs to hear it, but because she feels a need to share it with someone, and because she feels more inclined to offer such a confidence to this lanky throat-knobbed tech worker than to anyone among her science colleagues. It's a feeling which has manifested frequently for her these past few days.

Enough of reverie. There's work to be done. She nudges the featherweed further out away from the airship, a duckling testing the waters beyond the immediate purview of its ever-watchful, dramatically-oversized mother duck. She's manoeuvring towards the kilometre-broad gulf between the closest pair of zeps, at a range of slightly more than five kilometres from the *Wayfaring Stranger*. It's a slow, cautious, and slightly tedious process: she's purposely adopting a lazy haphazard flight that takes enough advantage of the fickle local air currents to avoid eliciting the zeps' suspicion (or so she hopes).

But if, for now, her activities have eluded the zeps' attention, they haven't escaped Sanna's. The plant behaviourist, who is for now the lab's only other occupant, appears to be waiting on some ostensibly uncooperative results of her own, and appears also to have decided that the most useful action to take in the interim is to engage Solveig in conversation. In consequence, Solveig finds herself on the receiving end of a soliloquy on the intricacies and subtleties of chemical signalling processes within the upper atmosphere, and the sharp distinction which can be drawn with analogous processes below the haze-deck, a distinction recognised, in large part, due to the analyses of Sanna herself, and—

It's interesting enough, Solveig supposes, trying not to get visually distracted by the petite botanist's carefully shaped monobrow. She should appreciate the company of Sanna, who's older, not fiercely competitive, and who has made much more effort than any other of her new colleagues in seeking to include Solveig within the labspace's sometimes hermetic, sometimes claustrophobic culture. And yet, with all her *so what is it you're hoping to achieve with your time here* and her *so you've worked with Xiaomei too how did you find her I thought she had some interesting ideas* and her *you must let me know if you need anything I know a new environment can sometimes feel daunting*, with all her busy friendliness and her sometimes too thorough efforts at social measurement, she's rubbed Solveig wrong: she's overly talkative, stands too close, makes eye contact at the wrong times. As though after fifty years it's something she's still trying to master.

Sanna's spiel sparks within Solveig a connection she's not properly able to articulate, some parallel with the ponderous zeps' surprising skittishness, their unpredictability. And she's always pleased, somewhat, to encounter someone so passionate about knowledge, and about the process of understanding. But listening to Sanna is not what Solveig wants to be doing right now. It's too all-consuming, too demanding. And her regular and overt glances in the direction of the featherweed's monitors do not seem to be sending a clear enough signal…

She feels like a hypocrite. Her unvoiced complaint of the past few weeks has been that her lab-space colleagues have held themselves aloof, have isolated or marginalised her; but even though Sanna is openly including her, she finds herself resenting the intrusion. (But if Sanna is looking to make this a dialogue rather than an oral presentation, she's clearly taking the long way about it. Solveig's few attempts to steer the discussion onto her own work invariably lead back to the chemistries of attractants and repellents, and of the almost supernatural sensitivity of some Rousseauvian species to the slightest gradients of key bioactive trace components. Even the lepidoptera, she is told, famous among terrestrial organisms for their ability to navigate long distances towards minutely heightened concentrations of sex pheromones, are by comparison untalented in this regard.)

Solveig suggests coffee, not so much from any immediate personal need for caffeination as in the hope that a change in scene might interrupt Sanna's barely-disguised discourse. It doesn't, really, but somehow it seems less disrespectful to be staring out the rec lounge window and nodding or humming agreement to the other's commentary than it would be to be similarly perusing the featherweed's monitor display back in the lab. (She wonders if she has, perhaps, another reason also for having wanted to break for coffee, but there's no-one other than the two of them in the rec lounge and, in truth, she's not sure she wouldn't have been uncomfortable if he *had* been there.)

She's sitting closer to the viewscreen than would normally be her preference—she's not good with heights, but Sanna seems to have a definite seating preference—which ensures she can see further up into the dazzlingly bright upper reaches than she can from her normal vantage within the lounge. Much of what she can see looking up is, of course, the *Wayfaring Stranger*'s envelope, but against the almost-luminous fringe of sky that hangs in her field of view just below the envelope's edge, there are two or three lozenge-shaped silhouettes that can only be additional zeps riding several kilometres higher than those which have congregated in the airship's vicinity. And now, belatedly, she knows what all this behaviour signifies: an event that's been documented before, but always only at a considerable distance.

If the zeps do not all decide to move on in the next few days …

Solveig stands, pushing her chair back with a noisy scrape against the flooring. Sanna has, of course, been saying something—is still saying something—but Solveig hasn't heard a word of the past several sentences. Her heart is thumping with pure excitement. 'I have to get back to the lab,' she explains, and she bustles away without waiting for the xenobotanist.

She hasn't even finished her coffee.

Daycycle 43, pre-shift / WS-352.78R

She needs more eyes out there. So she starts fabricating another two featherweeds, all the while monitoring the night-vision feed from the first one. The hoped-for zep activity doesn't eventuate, nor has there yet been much in the way of the zep vocalisation and visual display she'd been hoping to capture with the featherweed's deployment, but she cannot shake the thrum of suspended excitement that has hung with her since that realisation in the rec lounge with Sanna. She labours over the new probes all the rest of the day, connecting, testing, reshaping, keeping a weather eye on the monitors as she works. The assembly should be more straightforward the second time around—she has the specifications of the prototype device on hand—but she finds herself making irritating, clumsy errors. She forces herself to walk away from the still-incomplete builds as evening falls, and as Bao and Rewi enter the lab animatedly discussing their recent results.

She's in an odd mood: fizzy about the zeps, grumpy about the half-assembled featherweeds, annoyed at herself for very belatedly realising that Sanna was perhaps trying not merely to make conversation, nor to impose expertise, but to advise her about how best to make the featherweed's motions appear natural and unprogrammed. She feels a little shaky. *Is that nerves, or just a consequence of a missed lunch?* She's not sure.

She climbs the aft ladder up to the self-serve. It's definitely nerves, because the first person she sees as she enters the room is Liam, seated with the Trade crew, trading banter. She must look like an idiot, staring like this, cheeks starting to flame; but he turns his face towards her, smiles, says something she can't catch to Isis sitting next to him, stands up. Walks towards Solveig.

'Long day,' he says, inclining his head towards the nearest window. As if to say *what's out there has been keeping you busy.*

'Yes,' she says, wanting to meet those eyes, but somehow catching her gaze on that Adam's apple. She wonders, idly, if she'd be able to persuade him to wear something with a high neck. The thought does nothing for the blush on her cheeks; at least, nothing to abate it. 'Are you—'

'I've already eaten.'

'Oh,' she replies, and somehow the sole syllable is so blatantly crestfallen that she wants to kick herself.

'But I'm happy to wait while you get something for yourself,' he says.

'I'm a slow eater,' she confesses, moving towards the servery. 'I don't want to hold you up.'

'I don't have any plans,' he says.

'Me neither,' she allows. Tells herself she's done with featherweeds for the day, and done, too, with her labspace colleagues. She's silent for a half-minute, making her selections from a menu she already knows to encompass a not entirely adequate variety of fare, then leads him to an empty table. 'So tell me all about *your* day,' she says as she takes her seat.

She listens, interestedly enough. It turns out she's not such a slow eater as she's made out. But something about the meal disagrees with her, or perhaps it's a consequence of the indecision that's been building within her all day, as closely connected, she now sees, with Liam as it is with the zep situation. She likes Liam; she's clear on that point, is sufficiently self-honest to own the awareness. But she has no wish, in short, to repeat the mistake she feels she made with Herrick. It's this thought, at least as much as the gastric unsettlement that provides the more diplomatic pretext for curtailing this conversation with him. It doesn't, of course, assuage her own unease at doing so: he's broken off an interaction with his colleagues to spend time with her, and she's retreating to her room.

It's not the signal she *wants* to send…

He seems understanding, even concerned. Which is sweet, all told, but complicates her feelings further. She forces herself to avoid the thyroid stare as she bids him good evening, and leaves, not for her room, as she has planned, but back to the labspace.

Nothing is ever simple, she tells herself, without even fully knowing what she means by it.

It is, she reflects wryly, an odd complaint to be articulated by someone who has made it her vocation to decipher the communicative behaviour of aliens.

Daycycle 44, shift 1 / WS-353.06R

While there is only one zep within observable range, it's merely The Zep, no other identification required. The arrival of a second or third zep scarcely changes this: it (she) instead becomes That Zep, or The Zep Lying Nearly Due East, or something similarly and as simply descriptive. But with proliferation have come problems, and Solveig refuses to adopt the biologists' recommended syntax of 'Study Object WS-352.37R/Zep01', 'Study Object WS-352.62R/Zep02', *et cetera*, regardless of how historically useful such notation might ultimately prove to be. These creatures are individually distinct: she requires a system of naming which acknowledges this, which confers upon them names in some measure befitting their significance, their particularity. They do not, of course, require human names at all, and indeed no purely human name can be entirely justified; but she needs to call them something which properly distinguishes each of them, which does not demean entities who might well fully be her equal, or who exceed that—upon whatever scale one might wish to seek balance on such an issue. She settles, ultimately, on the named South Pacific temperate cyclones of the 2328/2329 season: Ava, Berit, Colwyn, Dien, Emeric, Feryal, Gajendra, Harper, Inari, Jauhera, Kibbe, Lirit. They're no more suitable than would be any other name, but she is pleased to have delegated accountability for their selection to an individual, committee, or organisation that can be safely assumed to have long since expired.

Having allocated a sequence of names, assigned for the order in which the zeps were first observed, she must properly learn to identify them. With a nonsentient creature, physical tagging of some form might be the preferred approach, but the few previous encounters between human researchers and zeps have established that this technique is counterproductive. Recognition must instead depend upon close observation and the gradual identification of individuating features: the wounds, blemishes and slightly protruding blebs which may or may not mark each creature's hide; the number and placement around the zep's 'envelope' of its attendant remoras; the sizes, shapes and coloration of each individual's mouths, olfactory trenches, craterous auditory receptors, genitoexcretory sphincters, and miscellaneous nubs and freckles of an as-yet-undetermined but presumably orientational or sensory purpose. Complicating this observational task are the factors that the zeps are Janus-like, dual-faced, as befits such a large and comparatively unmanoeuvreable creature, and with mouths placed on the same line as each pair of eyes can as effectively appear upside down as right way up. Nor, except in the grossest sense, is size of substantial value in discriminating between individuals lacking any form of skeletal rigidity and whose defining physical characteristic, in contrast, might be considered to be inflatability. It helps, of course, that they do not move rapidly; nonetheless, Solveig must expend a significant amount of time, at each daycycle's start, in verifying that the specimens occupying broadly-similar locations to those in which she last observed them are indeed those which she expects, since it is not always the case.

Daycycle 45, shift 2 / WS-353.38R
Something's afoot, out in the distant mid-morning air; she's seen it from the lounge viewport, and indeed it's this glimpse which has dragged her back to her bench. The featherweed is almost optimally placed, though,

as it transpires, awkwardly oriented: trained to maintain the closest zep in the centre of its broad field of view, its semi-smart controller has apparently yet to fully assimilate the difference between 'zep' and '*Wayfaring Stranger*'. She spends two to three minutes slowly gyring the probe to starboard, wondering a-mutter all the while as to how hard can it be to keep a creature with a major axis of a quarter kilometre within view…

The behaviour she's seeking to capture is something she's been waiting for, these past days: a substantial and sustained interaction between zeps. Seven kilometres due east of the airship, two zeps, Inari and Kibbe, are facing off against each other, across a gulf of barely half a kilometre; in zep terms, almost touching. The communication between them is silent, or nearly so: Solveig cannot be certain whether the slight growls the featherweed is picking up are zep-initiated, or even if so whether they represent genuine vocalisation or perhaps merely the sound of some autonomous or low-order physiological process connected to digestion, buoyancy maintenance, or attitude control.

Zep chameleonism is as little studied a phenomenon as any other aspect of the creatures' communication. It's known that the zeps are highly adept at stippling their flanks with more or less irregular blotches of subtly or even vividly contrasting colours, but what purpose this serves isn't known. Sexual signalling? Claim of territoriality? An alert to danger? Solveig's fairly sure, watching this pair, that in this case at least it's none of these; but she can't believe, in this instance, it is anything more prosaically conversational either. These flankside displays would be scarcely visible from directly ahead, so it seems less probable that this is dialogue rather than commentary for the benefit of others watching. It's as if each of the zep pair is seeking to outdo the other in display: Inari remains as utterly static as is possible for an untethered gas-filled creature in a mildly turbulent atmosphere, while the patterning of off-white lozenges and concave-sided diamond shapes on its whale-blue hide rotates like a drum around its girth. At the same time, Kibbe physically matches the pattern of the other's rotation, while keeping its own Ben Day-dotted hide seemingly motionless, an illusion belied by the steadily shifting orientation of its large-eyed, gape-mouthed face, and of its cohort of carefully-attached remoras.

It's stunning to watch; it's deeply alien.

They're playing, Solveig thinks. *It's a display of skill, for their own amusement or to pass the time, or to impress others watching…* but all of this is guesswork, nothing sure, perhaps nothing ever knowable. It's so difficult to know which of the concepts she carries as the rudiments of her science are genuinely applicable to such creatures, and which are of merely human, or vertebrate, or even terrestrial relevance, and not even her experience with the taniwha can genuinely be viewed as instructive here. Zeps are different; and she can't even know how different that might be. *If I could only get out there, take a hand in attempting to converse with them. Provoke a response. Measure their reaction. It likely still wouldn't help, but it would feel like progress. I'd feel less of a curator.*

On a technical level, on an observational level, the feed she's getting from the probe is useful, even valuable: the featherweed is substantially closer to the zeps than would ever be any human-crewed craft, and well equipped to garner measurements and observations. But as to the furtherance of her ambition to comprehend the inner workings and outward expression of the zep mentality (as though there can even be any such homogenous concept among creatures who very likely have distinct if incomprehensible individual personalities), she is still, in all practical respects, operating in darkness. An accumulation of observed behaviours, of vocalisation and chameleonism and what might pass, in zep parlance, for 'body language' may ultimately prove useful in unravelling the fabric of zep communication, but without some unguessable stimulus, some hit of insight, it remains likely to be an exceptionally slow process.

It keeps me busy, she tells herself. *And if my contribution is ultimately sufficient to assist the broader scientific community in establishing what we would consider 'contact' with these creatures, without my own role itself necessarily proving pivotal, then should that not be enough? For me?*

She's not sure that it is. And it's this that's the problem, and this that has her again feeling discommoded when, after two full hours of studious perusal of the featherweed feed to the near-complete exclusion of whatever sporadically taint-leaking modes of investigation Rewi and Torsten have been up to at their respective containment chambers, she calls a halt and takes herself off to the not entirely satisfactory solitude of her quarters for the necessity of sleep, or of at least its attempt.

four

Daycycle 50, intershift / WS-354.59R

She eyes the ladderway without favour. Liam in exercise kit is not a problem: nice legs, a scent of mildly stale sweat that, somehow, is not as off-putting as she usually finds such things. And she's at peace, approximately, with her own sartorial concessions towards physical fitness. But she doesn't see why the *Wayfaring Stranger* couldn't have a gymnasium, even a small one, somewhere within its multilevel gondola; something tidily contained, in preference to… this.

'You look ill at ease, Doc,' he comments, right hand on a rung that is, for him, slightly more than head-high.

'I'm fine,' she lies, looking up to meet the hatchway's stare.

'It does take some getting used to.'

'Liam, I'm *fine*. Can we just get on with it?'

'You're the boss.' He ascends two rungs, presses the access contact. The hatchway slides open with an unnerving rasp and a hardly less disconcerting waft of sulfide. He climbs into the airlock, steps onto the creaking interlocking C-fibre plates that tesselate its decking, gazes down to where she stands still looking up at this opening in the gondola's ceiling.

'You're sure this is safe?' she asks, unable to fully hide her uncertainty as she begins to climb.

'As safe as anything is,' he replies. 'They had glass-windowed passenger

"

cabins within the envelopes of the early twentieth-century airships. This isn't that different.'

'Those airships didn't generally end well,' she says, climbing into the lock, trying not to give in to… not claustrophobia, exactly; nothing so clear-cut as panic; but a distinct if ill-defined sense of apprehension, as the airlock hatch slides closed beneath them.

The lock, its bowed walls and upper surface clad in some semi-elastic polymer of an uninspiringly dirty beige, is poorly lit by footlights in the chamber's corners, with only a rudimentary and badly-tarnished control panel set into the wall beside the outer vertical hatch. Solveig strives to quell the biochemical rebellion that seems to be brewing somewhere in her midriff while Liam, unconcerned, pads casually at the control panel's uppermost button. 'Technologies mature, Doc. Early heavier-than-airs weren't that safe either, nor early spacecraft, nor the first implants. But there hasn't been a fatality involving airships in over a century.'

'On Earth,' she notes.

'On Earth,' he agrees. The hatch has irised open, revealing a T-shaped junction with a tubular passageway, a chain of the footlights stretching off, in both directions, into the distance. The corridor looks as though it must extend further than the confines of the envelope which contains it, though she knows this to be impossible. There's a low atonal whistle, rising and ebbing in volume: the eerie, otherworldly, ever-patient sigh of Rousseau's atmosphere, pushing or tugging against the *Wayfaring Stranger*'s envelope. This is the sound—or more accurately, merely one of the sounds—she's been sequestered from for the past several weeks, by the gondola's quad-laminar viewports and efficiently-insulated hull.

She fancies she can feel the airlock flex around her.

She grows aware that Liam, standing by the two-metre-wide aperture, is waiting for her to step through. She feels sick; she is comprehensively beyond every self-identified safe limit; but she agreed to this, and she's obligated to follow through.

The floor of the trackway tubing is less disconcertingly pneumatic than she has been expecting—she has to concentrate, in fact, to convince herself that there is any discernible flexion of the walking surface—but it's still an effort to take each individual step.

She's enclosed, she's supported, but she doesn't believe it. It's just a skin of nondescript polymer.

Behind her, the airlock hatch slides closed once more. She stops, after ten paces, reminded with sudden force of an episode from her childhood back on Earth, when she had walked across the frozen surface of the lake behind her uncle's winter retreat. Her palms grow damp as she recalls the sensation of helpless terror, the awareness of the doom beneath her from which she was separated by only a thin crust, scarcely more than a membrane of unreliable early-season ice.

She can't turn back. That is just not an option. But she's highly unsure whether she possesses the spirit to proceed.

Liam, too, has stopped. She scans his face for signs of contempt or condescension or amusement, but there are none.

'Whenever you're ready, Doc,' he offers, gesturing with his upturned palm towards the distant end of the running-tube.

'Okay,' she replies. 'But you lead, please? And don't worry about the pace; I'm actually quite fast.'

Fast she may be, but she's also out of practice. The muscles in her sides are beginning to ache with lactic acid overload by the time they reach the first hairpin bend in the four-hundred-metre loop of tube, as it circumscribes the base of the envelope within which it's embedded. She stops and signals for Liam to do likewise.

She looks back the way they've come. The dingy elasticised tunnel, three metres in width, appears impossibly long, interrupted only by emergency breathing-apparatus recesses every fifty metres and by a regular sequence of occasionally faulty footlights. She and Liam follow the curve around at little more than walking pace. She fancies she can feel the running tube, perhaps the entire voluminous envelope of the airship, dip in response to her footfalls, so far from the *Wayfaring Stranger*'s own centre of gravity; tells herself it's likely only her overclocked imagination. She tries not to think about how little substance stands between herself and asphyxiation, inhalation of toxic gas, the combustible admixture of the tunnel's oxygenated air with the envelope's vast reserves of hydrogen, and a sixteen-kilometre fall through alien air. She tries, therefore, to take her lead from Liam, who's fine with all of this. She envies that. She *wants* that. She enjoys Liam's company, his innate comfort with his surroundings; she wants to overcome her fears.

The things she wants to ask Liam are not the things she can raise with him, not yet. So instead, once her heart and lungs have settled (and after he and she have fast-walked for what subjectively feels to have been a couple of minutes, yet has not ostensibly brought the visible end-wall curve of the running tube any closer), she says, 'Hong scares me shitless.'

It's something she can't say to any of her colleagues: it would be ammunition. But she needs to say it to *someone*, and her sense is that Liam is substantially the safest person within a dozen kilometres in whom she can confide such an observation.

If she's wrong in that assumption, then she's just made a dangerous mistake.

Liam doesn't answer straightaway, and when he does, it's with such a guarded 'Why do you say that?' that it does very little to quell her unease at having overstepped some professional boundary.

She takes her own time responding. 'I guess I find her impossible to read. I mean, she comes across as very severe, but I find myself thinking that might just be a front.'

'I don't have much to do with her,' replies Liam. 'I'm not in her line of responsibility. But from what I've heard you read her just fine. Didn't you force her hand on keeping the ship embedded in the zep field?'

'Zep field?'

'That's what Cordero calls it. He's the one with primary navigational responsibility. Said he'd heard you'd outmanoeuvred the Director quite effectively.'

'That wasn't what I was trying to do—I just wanted Hong to see the substance of my interest in the zeps, and to understand the magnitude of the opportunity this … congregation gives us. Did that come from

Hong, that I forced her hand?'

'Probably from the Captain, unless Cordero's thing with Torsten is on again,' says Liam. 'Which I don't think it is.'

'Shit,' says Solveig. 'I mean, forced her hand, that's a fairly loaded term.'

'I wouldn't worry about it. She agreed, didn't she?'

'Yes, but I never wanted anything so… adversarial. I had enough of that at the lake station.'

'Is that this business with Jens that you've mentioned?'

'Pretty much. I guess I'm just not that good with authority. Which is not a useful characteristic for someone in my line of work.'

'Is there a line of work for which it is?' Liam asks, the reply quick enough that she can't completely stifle a snort of amusement.

'Anyway,' she says, after spending a few seconds trying to think of a smart reply. 'I don't think I want to keep talking about that at the moment. Let's find some other topic.'

'Such as?'

'I was just thinking … You know what this tube needs?'

'A handrail?' he asks.

She digs him playfully in the ribs with her elbow, then regrets her own forwardness. 'No. A panoramic display, something wraparound.'

'We've got that in the rec lounge. Or near enough,' he replies.

'No, not Rousseau, that's all around us anyway, I mean something that would be—not an escape, that's not quite what I'm driving at, but a distraction, something—'

'So if it was you,' he asks, 'what would you choose, for this panorama? This distraction?'

She delays her answer; she hasn't really thought this through. 'North Ontario. The lakeshore behind my uncle's farm, an old boardwalk and marshes and loons hiding behind a stand of reeds. You?'

'Are you homesick?' Liam asks her. They've reached the prow bend in the tube.

She's not intending to stop, but she does anyway. The question has caught her unawares, with such an odd emphasis on the word that she's not sure how to take it. Is there approbation in his phrasing? 'Not... no, I don't think I would say that,' she responds at last. 'Just, I suppose, a bit nostalgic.' And then spends the next hundred metres wondering whether there is indeed any distinction to be made between the concepts. 'You?' she asks.

'Valles Marineris,' he replies, then describes exactly which small stretch of the vast canyon he has in mind.

It's only after they negotiate the decision to make another two circumnavigations of the track—Solveig would just as soon not, but she knows four hundred metres scarcely counts as exercise—that she realises he hasn't really answered the question she'd asked.

She elects not to pursue it.

Daycycle 50, shift 2 / WS-354.62R

'It's not your concern,' she protests, both bewildered and furious that this exchange is happening—quietly, to be sure, but happening nonetheless—within the far-from-private confines of the rec lounge, rather than within Hong's office alcove. If, indeed, it needs to occur at all. She can't help thinking that this is payback, or something similar, for her earlier intervention on the *Wayfaring Stranger*'s scheduled course.

'I disagree,' replies Hong, her eyebrows tensed down in what Solveig has started to suspect is a near-permanent frown. 'It is exactly my concern. You were seconded here under my supervision, and that makes it my concern. Just as Junior Officer Subramanian serves under Captain Gill's supervision and is therefore her concern. So a dalliance between the two of you—'

'It's not a dalliance!' Solveig responds, feeling her face flush. She hasn't even had a chance to change out of her exercise kit. 'My apologies, Director Hong, I did not intend to raise my voice. But Liam and I are adults, and entirely professional individuals fully capable of responsible action regardless of the circumstances. At least, I know this about myself, and I think I can reliably say it of him also. You're treating us, treating me like, like, I don't know, like some kind of junior-educational-facility—'

'I am treating you as a member of a team,' Hong says, 'within a small human-habitable lighter-than-air vessel stationed between fifteen and twenty kilometres' altitude within the non-breathable atmosphere of an alien planet, on which human outposts of any kind are very far and few between. Under such circumstances, given the difficulty, danger, and expense involved in any staffing changes required, it's my responsibility as science manager to ensure that no situation develops which threatens team harmony. A corrosive end to an interpersonal relationship can constitute such a threatening situation within the cramped confines we work in that your sinecure here might need to be annulled. Now I could instruct you to end whatever interaction has sprung up between you and Subramanian—'

'I wouldn't do it,' Solveig says, her dander now properly up. 'That is to say, I'd give you an assurance that I would do so, if that was the price of remaining on board, but I wouldn't actually do it, because it's not reasonable and it's not necessary and it's not practical and it *really is not any of your fucking business,* Director.' She turns to stare out the rec lounge's viewscreen, counts to twelve. Turns back towards her supervisor. 'My apologies. But I think it's best if at least one of us speaks plainly. Are you going to push this… this preposterous interventionism any further? Are you going to tell me my time on board the airship is up, tell me here in public in the rec lounge, because of some ludicrous, nebulous concern for the group dynamics that, really, I thought we as a society had grown out of? Or am I free to retire to my quarters, to use my free time as I see fit?'

'You admit the relationship,' notes Hong.

'Actually, I don't,' says Solveig. 'I just object with every molecule of my being to the attitude you're taking, to the threats you've bewilderingly decided to level against me. There is a friendship between Liam and I, Liam and me rather, and that is not a bad thing. It is not necessarily any more than that. Nor is it a thing you need interfere in.'

'Solveig,' Hong replies mildly, sounding as surprised to be uttering the name as Solveig herself is to be hearing it from this small, insular, severe woman who has had the mantle of administration foisted upon her storied academic core. 'Of course I am not going to push, at this stage, for the termination of your research position here on board. You came to us very highly recommended, and everything I've seen of your efforts in development of the zep communication project leads me to believe that that recommendation was not in error. I am very keen, from both a professional and a personal curiosity-driven perspective, to see what you accomplish during your time here. But I am already starting to suspect that you are not the team player that you described yourself as in your application for the position you now hold. A commitment to team safety and team coherence is every bit as important, more important in some respects, than any individual research outcomes or social interactions. You must understand my overriding concern, which stems from my responsibility for the sum total of all research carried on onboard, just as Captain Gill is responsible for—'

'Yes, I got that,' says Solveig, once she's past the shock of this talk of recommendation. *It must have been Jens*, she thinks. *Nobody else's input would've carried enough weight with the adjudicators. But Jens was looking to screw me over, she just needed a scapegoat for the messy end to the taniwha station's work, and I fitted the frame.* 'I still don't see any grounds for you to believe that whatever might pass between us, between Liam and I, should be the least business of yours. It's presumptuous, it's inappropriate, it's invasive—'

'I'm not directly concerned with any relationship between yourself and Subramanian. It's the possible consequences. What happens on board is larger, more important than any one or two of us. I just wish you to keep that awareness central to your worldview while you call this research station your home. The upper atmosphere is no place for caprice.'

'Noted,' says Solveig, striving to get through the distancing filter through which she seems to be hearing her manager's words. She needs not to feel that this encounter is happening to someone else, rather than herself. She needs her wits about her for this conversation, not this adrenalised, tinnitus-steeped bullshit that her body has autonomously thrust upon her. 'But frankly—'

'I'm not talking about everyday irritations,' Hong explains. 'Intense emotions can fester when two people suddenly find themselves on opposite sides of the question about how they view the other. I need to avoid the risk of impulsive action, inattention, or interpersonal conflict, and the danger that presents to those onboard. I require you to notify me without hesitation if any serious rift develops between you and Subramanian, so I can ensure onboard safety.'

'Noted.'

'I'm sure you feel that this reprimand, this warning, on my part is an overreaction.'

Solveig shakes her head, purely because to nod in agreement at this stage would not serve her purpose.

'I can assure you,' Hong continues, 'that it is not. I've seen such things occur, and the closed environment of a long-duration research mission is not one I can willingly place at risk of such… hazards.' There's something cold, something challenging, in her stare accompanying these words, alongside some tic that Solveig interprets as a twitch of vulnerability.

Who hurt you? she wonders. She wants to look away, but forces herself to meet the defensively furrowed brow and mid-brown eyes of the science cluster manager who may, Solveig suspects, be younger than she is herself, for all of Hong's reputation as an exceptionally astute researcher and academic. *Who hurt you, what did they break within you, and why do you feel the need to seek redress in this way? Am I that much of a nuisance, an inconvenience to you? Is this payback for my having 'forced your hand', as Liam put it? Or is it that I remind you of some part of yourself that you feel now lies dormant, subservient, or dead within you?* But she can say none of this, of course. Instead she merely asks, with all the outward calm she can muster, 'Are we done?'

'We're done,' says Hong. 'Thank you for hearing to my concerns.'

'Noted.' Solveig, turning, glares at Bao who has been seated across the lounge this entire time, unable to avoid hearing what their colleagues have been discussing. She makes her escape.

*

There are voices ahead, somewhere around the bend. Rewi? Sanna? She can't determine; the tubeway's acoustics are poor.

She's breathing quick and shallow, thoughts a-whirl through her head, fists clenched as she paces her way around the tubeway, too furious to recollect just what about this space had her so unnerved the previous time, those few hours ago. She's angry at Hong; at herself for not having handled it better; at Jens for not having stood up for her, back at the lake station.

Quick steps. Keep moving. Adrenalise the anger away.

She needs this time to herself. She's glad, now, of this intimidating long loop of inflated tubing, this expanse within an otherwise stiflingly confining environment. Hopes she can keep apace enough of whoever it is up ahead to preserve the sense of solitude; she has no wish to be lapped, no wish even to be seen. For a while, perhaps for as much as a kilometre—she doesn't trust her curve-counting sufficiently to be sure of the distance—she rehearses in her mind the process of resigning her secondment here, of farewelling the *Wayfaring Stranger*. It's a bitter plan, and it doesn't last. Not because of Liam; not because to resign would be to hand Hong a quite undeserved and petty victory; but because of the zeps.

I will take this as far as I fucking can, she tells herself. *She doesn't get to control me. I should've made that clear back at the lake station, with Jens, but now is soon enough. A breakthrough with the zeps probably won't happen unless they cooperate with us towards it, and they probably won't. But I deserve the chance to make the effort.*

In the end it's thirst, rather than the ebbing of stamina, nerve, or anger, that forces her descent back into the cramped society of the gondola. By her own unreliable estimation, she has walked at least eight kilometres around the tubeway; it may be as many as ten.

'It's not how I'd imagined,' she says, lying beside Liam on her technically too-narrow-for-two sleeping surface, in her small room. They're still, at this point, fully clothed—footwear excepted—and she's not entirely sure this isn't a mistake, more despite Hong's concerns than because of them. (She senses Liam's not entirely sure either. Has he received, from Captain Gill, a cousin of the imprecation to which Hong subjected her, those few hours ago?) She *likes* Liam—likes him a lot—but she's keenly aware that he's the closest thing to a friend she's found on the *Wayfaring Stranger*, so the potential for emotional pain, and for ongoing difficulty if she messes this up, is high indeed. An airship gondola's not a large space. 'Up here, I mean,' she adds, aware that she's allowed the silence to linger long enough to become awkward. She flexes her hip and props herself up on one elbow, achieving three things: one, she gains relief from Liam's belt buckle, which has been awkwardly pressed against the base of her abdomen; two, she is now looking *over* rather than staring directly *at* Liam's Adam's apple (and when, if what they have ever turns out to be a relationship, will it be acceptable to mention to him that this feature of his has always bugged her?); three, she has a distinctly better view out the room's porthole, where just now the vista is incredible. 'When I was groundside, preparing to come up here, I knew it'd be different, but …'

'How d'you mean, Doc?' Liam asks. She's mildly staggered that he's facing her, rather than trying to catch the sunset as she is. Even if he has perhaps seen it a hundred times before.

'Down there, in the cold and the darkness, you almost forget that there's another side to the planet. I spent three years at the lakeside station, and we lived our lives under shadow. The most I saw of the sun was as a smudge in the midday haze. So of course I thought, *Wayfaring Stranger*, riding above the haze-deck, bright sunlight: I'd be seeing the sun a lot, wouldn't I? I'd been forgetting about the ship's envelope. The only times I see the sun are at sunrise and sunset.'

'Actually, that's partly down to the way the ship's oriented at the moment. If we were north/south instead of east/west, you'd be getting more sun.'

'So why are we east/west?'

'Prevailing winds. And solar energy.' He grins, places an almost feather-light hand on her raised shoulder. 'But I thought you said we weren't to talk shop.'

'I did, didn't I? But I'd hardly call that shop.'

'It may not be shop for you. It's shop for me.'

She slides down, meeting his gaze. 'Okay, tell me something non-shop.'

So he does. The details needn't concern us.

Daycycle 51, early / WS-354.76R

Night falls—or rather, it seems to Solveig, night rises like a languidly dimming extension of the haze-deck, swallowing the upper air within its dark maw. And yet, as the sky's highlights ebb from orange into dull crimson-grey and brown, sparse and unpredictable episodes of phosphorescence erupt. Full night will see the sky indeed turn quite dark, but the first several hours after dusk are a time of high activity, and strange beauty.

'How can you not take in that view?' she asks.

'There'll be other opportunities to look out portholes,' he replies, and smiles.

I could quite fall for you, Liam Subramanian, she tells herself, pulling him closer.

five

Daycycle 53, shift 1 / WS-355.30R

It's an exercise in pattern-matching and interpretation, and at this stage it seems fruitless. She has four daycycles—nine probe-daycycles—eight hundred and ninety-four cam-hours—of useful data to peruse, and more accruing by the hour. Because of the timing of the featherweed probes' releases, the majority of the footage is night vision; but a fresh Rousseau day has dawned, so this will change. Keeping atop of the surveillance is not a task she can ever hope to surmount unassisted, but the automated systems are stumbling in as much of a conceptual haze as is she. The necessary precursor is to map the details of zep behaviour; to ascertain which signals, which responses, accompany which stimuli; and then to hazard a causal, a conscious, connection between them. To draw parallels between creatures who might well be expected to be every bit as idiosyncratic and as stubbornly individual as humans, and who collectively are nothing like any terrestrial lifeform.

It would be difficult enough if the zeps wanted *to initiate communication with us. Without that ambition on their part, it's an unreasonably uphill struggle. If they won't make it, the effort falls only on us.*

The zeps are, for now, unfathomable; but they are as mortal and as biochemical as any other creature. There must be some way through to them. Or is to hold such an aspiration to reduce them to the status of enigma, when they are assuredly something so much more complex?

The zeps have a quarter-kilometre major axis and scant means of lateral propulsion, which means that not much happens quickly. That said, though, they're never entirely still: there's drift, there's roll, there's the play of changing colour across their flanks. They graze; they respire; they excrete; they orient themselves in alignment with, or opposition to, the changing currents. And it's not possible to know whether the important shifts in their interactions with the sky, and with the other zeps distantly clustered around them, are the sparse episodes of sudden reorientation, or the slow and subtle transitions. It all must be mapped, it all must be correlated, it all must be sifted for chance wisps of relevance, of potential xenolinguistic value. The challenge of it, in some sense, is enjoyable, rewarding; but the likelihood that her progress will be minimal is spirit-sapping. She wants to know these creatures. And so, attention switching between the live feed from the featherweeds' cams and the steadily extending backlog of data awaiting cataloguing (or at least perusal), she spends a draining, busy morning seated at her bench, hoping for a persistently elusive transcendence from busywork into enlightenment, oblivious to the sporadic bustle of her colleagues' activities in the labspace around her, and to the sour suggestion of bloon decomposition leaking through the nanopores of Bao's biocontainment booth. She rises from her stool only when the tension of sitting immobile for such a span has triggered a briefly agonising cramp in her left calf. Sensing her movement, the workbench elevates itself.

Time for coffee?

Sanna evidently thinks so, and she and Rewi depart for the rec lounge. Solveig demurs without really knowing why, knows only that she's not in a companionable mood.

Thinking like a zep, she tells herself. Smiles at the joke against herself: because truly she has no idea of what any zep thinks, or feels.

If she wants to understand the zeps, she must first comprehend them. She must be able to predict their behaviour in various circumstances. The human animal is a builder, a disruptor, a communicator, a deceiver, an envisioner, a collaborator, an opportunist, a controller, a questioner. All of these aspects Solveig carries within herself, to a greater or lesser extent than her compatriot star-flung primates: they inform her character, her reflexes, her conscious responses. Knowing this, she can interpret those around her, just as they can interpret (or misinterpret) her: this is the subtext of human discourse. But what holds here, atop Rousseau's primary haze layer, amidst creatures encased around vast sacs of hydrogen? It's a line of inquiry she's repeatedly attempted to plumb, these past weeks, and it has never yet led her to any insight sufficient to constitute real progress in her quest.

Nonetheless, the process remains. Measure. Record. Correlate. Catalogue. The observations are valuable for their own sake, as a foundation for further work, even if she cannot bring any useful shine to the data.

The zep grouping provides an opportunity to get a foothold on zep communication. These are creatures that will communicate with each other, even if they shun the effort of attempting to communicate with humans. But zep groupings of this type are vanishingly rare. Solveig's recording of this encounter, therefore, is not so distant in its scope from those pioneering flybys that allowed the measurement and mapping of previously unknown worlds, with data acquired in the brief frenzy of proximity and parcelled out over months or even years for transmission back to Earth. Her role, right now, is not to attempt to decipher, but simply to observe in as much exhaustive detail as she can, while the opportunity persists. Within the broader Rousseauvian research effort, within the science community on the *Wayfaring Stranger*, her duty for the moment is to act as a data-gatherer; not as a spinner of conjecture, a generator of hypotheses.

This doesn't keep her from thinking, of course.

What we'll be getting out of this, if we get anything, is an insight into the behaviour of a population of zeps; which is not the same thing as zep behaviour per se. *Is there a zep analogue of mob rule?*

But it's fruitless to cavil about such distinctions at this point. We need all the information we can get, and a gathering like this is at least as good a way as any to acquire that information.

Were I alien, and to monitor the interactions between a priest, a labourer, and a thief, I would learn more of humanity than if I were to observe only one of those. That seems an uncontroversial enough starting point, and one that should also be safely generalisable to zeps also.

But what occupations could persist among organisms without the means of propulsion and manipulation? Priest, perhaps, still; not labourer nor thief, but poet, philosopher, mathematician, counsellor, adjudicator, educator, explorer... and perhaps others, which have no counterpart among human society. It may be all of those, or none. And any one of these zeps within the Wayfaring Stranger's *purview might have one or other of those roles; if they are creatures that do, rather than creatures which just are. There's no straightforward way of knowing.*

But even if it transpired that they were so indolent, so purposeless as to make the most feckless wastrel second-son heir to a tycoon's unearned riches seem industrious by comparison... they'd still have to have distinct personalities, wouldn't they? Everything we know about intelligence more or less demands that. But what are those personalities? What distinguishes Ava from Berit, Colwyn from Dien? Why is the physical separation between Colwyn and Harper consistently several hundred metres less than that between Emeric and Feryal, when the latter two arrived more or less simultaneously, from the same direction, and the former pair migrated in on opposite headings a daycycle apart? What do they want from each other? Who are they?

Solveig doesn't know. She needs to know.

Rewi returns from the rec lounge with Torsten and Bao in tow. The solitude escapes the labspace, fleet as air through a cracked airlock, and with it her opportunity for reverie.

She returns to cataloguing. Some daycycles this is all there is.

Daycycle 53, aftershift / WS-355.42R

She shifts modes without ever being entirely clear, even within her own mind, as to why she's doing so.

Rousseau's diurnal cycle of almost one hundred and seventeen hours is an inconvenience for creatures acclimatised through a long-running process of natural selection to a twenty-four-hour cycle, and there is among the *Wayfaring Stranger*'s occupants a range of responses. While some among the scientists take a more or less stochastic attitude, working whatever span of hours appears at the time to be that expected from whatever phase their own research currently manifests, others operate on an approximately twenty-nine-hour cycle, populating each Rousseauvian day with four of their own: dawn, noon, dusk, midnight, or thereabouts. Solveig herself has fallen into this pattern since her arrival, several weeks past, on the airship. The tech officers, in contrast, are constrained by reason of the necessity of maintaining an orderly duty roster to follow a twenty-three-hour day length.

Solveig tells herself that the decision to adopt a shorter day length is a pragmatic one: she hasn't been sleeping particularly well since the zeps began to congregate, and fewer hours between shorter sleeps is a natural response to this inconvenience; it may also give her a better chance of intercepting any intriguing developments in the gathered zeps' interactions. But she's also aware that the shift also brings her into synchronisation with Liam's own pattern of days.

This is useful, in some respects, though it really is nothing more than coincidence.

Daycycle 54, mid-shift 1 / WS-355.53R
She's been seen. It would look odd to back out now. And she *does* need the coffee.

Solveig fills her mug, walks with what she suspects to be audible self-consciousness across the rec lounge, finds a seat at the farthest table. She'd prefer to be sitting with her back to them, but that would mean moving the chair and she has no wish to do anything so ostentatious. No wish to be doing anything that might suggest she's in any way focussed on the fact that Director Hong and Captain Gill are seated two tables away, heads bent in some private discussion.

I might as well have 'hypervigilant' etched in bioluminescent lettering across my forehead, she thinks. Tries to breathe normally. Tries not to appear frozen in her seat, or twitchy, or in any way awkward or uncomfortable. *Not going to win any awards for this performance.* She finds herself having to suppress a laugh at the thought.

She takes her coffee black; it takes a while to cool. Her thoughts go everywhere and nowhere, can find no purchase. Eventually one of the pair—she's not looking directly, so she can't even be sure which one—gets up and leaves the lounge. Solveig pushes down her coffee, still a few degrees too hot, and gets up to return her mug to the mag-tray. It's Gill who has departed, Hong who is still seated at the table, poring over some virtual data display or other. The manager looks up and nods as Solveig walks past her.

Does she know? Solveig can't help but ask herself. *And if so, is she biding her time? Or was that warning all just an act?*

Daycycle 57, shift 2 / WS-356.18R

The primary haze layer that blankets Rousseau's lower atmosphere is fashioned from, profits from, a quintillion small transactions every instant, as photons are absorbed, as bonds are formed, as configurations flex. So efficient are the haze layer's middleweight organics, branched-chain radicals and burgeoning nanoparticulate matter in the taxation of sunlight that scant luminosity remains unclaimed on its attempted traversal. But the haze does more than merely impose a perpetual state of near-total night on the domains beneath it: it also serves to quench any diurnal temperature variation. The surface is as blandly frigid as it is almost unvaryingly dark.

Above the haze deck, it's a different matter. Sunlight not only warms the upper atmosphere directly, through absorption and scattering, but also via heating of the haze-deck's upper reaches, which are consequently bright in infrared. The long night brings cooling, and a slight and gradual compaction of the air above the haze blanket. Buoyant lifeforms become less so, as their gaseous envelopes cool and contract and offer less lift to their encasements. Nighttime is feeding time for many of the heavier-than-air herbivores which, by day, coast on the thermals that form above the sun-warmed haze deck, and for numerous opportunistic predators and scavengers.

Zeps are sufficiently large and well-insulated that they do not appreciably lose heat, or buoyancy, during the stretch of hours between sunset and sunrise. Nighttime for them, too, is feeding time, and a time of enhanced activity. Most zep filter-feeding, most zep locomotion, occurs in darkness. Solveig finds herself wondering whether the zeps do not merely see the hours of daylight as a long and tedious interval between nights.

Put it on the list of questions to ask them. If they ever decide we're worth the effort of communication.

She's curled, rug-robed, upon the more comfortable of the rec lounge's two sedans, knees tented up and a viewpad nestled on her lap. The lounge, its windows opacified to ensure the lighting does not attract attention from some of the more sharp-snouted of the night's hunters, is quiet and warm and devoid, for now, of other human occupants, which suits Solveig well enough. She does not feel a need for the currently crowded labspace, nor of any of its equipment: from here, she can do all the analysis and monitoring and comparison that she needs, without interruption.

Why is it, she wonders, *that while I prefer solitude, I don't generally want to be alone?*

The question doesn't deeply concern her, it's just there. Hanging around. Like a zep.

Aside from musing on such imponderables, she's watching Jauhera. The battle-scarred zep is unmistakeable amongst an otherwise often-indistinguishable grouping of the gargantua: one face ostensibly blind, with milk-glazed eyes, and a flank marked by a set of long-healed dark gashes that, though never more than about twenty centimetres deep, extend in the longest instance for over eighty metres, fully a third of her length.

Such disfiguring stigmata might, to human eyes, suggest infirmity and an organism which has learnt, belatedly, to exercise caution; but Jauhera is notably the most actively mobile of those whom Solveig is keeping under surveillance, and has within the past few hours made almost seven kilometres' headway in a broadly north-westerly direction. Her purpose in doing so is not readily apparent: the flight is not taking her noticeably towards, nor directly away from, any other zep, it is not appreciably increasing the distance between her and the *Wayfaring Stranger*, it does not appear to be leading her through or into any notably rewarding feeding ground, nor can Solveig see anything overtly hazardous or threatening in the direction from which she is (in zep terms) racing. She's just a zep on the move.

Perhaps Jauhera has been spooked by something, but if this is the case, the danger is not detectable to Solveig's night-vision surveillance.

The extent of the time-weathered scarring on Jauhera's flank, and the damage to the face that the zep now apparently keeps consistently behind her, isn't something that has been recorded in any earlier zep sightings. This makes it unlikely that she has been the subject of close human study before this encounter, but in general it is never possible to know with anything approaching certainty whether a given zep has encountered human efforts at observation. The creatures have little in the way of identifiable permanent markings, and efforts to physically tag them have never succeeded: anything adhering to their dermis (remoras excepted) is rapidly sloughed off, while barbed markers are mysteriously disembedded within days of any such tagging. This might be the first time any of these zeps have encountered human researchers (or their proxies); it might be the sixth.

They must have a sense of identity, thinks Solveig. *Or at least of self; but surely they must also seek to determine the identity of those around them? Or perhaps such concerns do not matter to them in the way they do to us, or to the taniwha.*

If they do maintain continuity of recognition of one another, how is it achieved? Visually? Aurally? Behaviourally? Or through pheromones? Perhaps I should talk with Sanna…

She watches Jauhera plough open-mouthed through a small congregation of bloons, swallowing several; a few seconds later, the ingested air is energetically exhaled through the creature's other, currently rearward-facing mouth, pursed for what is presumably the greatest propulsive effect. Solveig doesn't think it's hunger which is provoking the zep's movement: this 'jet-feeding' is thought to require a much slower processing of the swallowed gas for an effective start to digestion. Rather, Jauhera is simply on the move, for purposes unknown.

Solveig decides to attempt something. She has the viewpad determine the periodicity of the zep's air-swallowing actions—a shade under ten seconds, based on a rapid analysis of the last several minutes' telemetry—and programs the featherweed most nearly in Jauhera's forward peripheral vision with instructions to repeatedly emit a flaring and fading visible-wavelength glow on the same deciHertz beat. *Conversation's too much to hope for; but a reaction of any kind might tell us something*, she tells herself. She's jeopardising the featherweed's cover, but assesses it as a risk worth taking. She suspects, in any case, that the zeps aren't fooled by the faked-out surveillance platforms, but are merely abiding their presence with the same indifferent tolerance they extend to the *Wayfaring Stranger*, provided it maintains its distance from them. The intervention's sole effect—if indeed it is the catalyst for that—is to cause the flank-scarred zep to deflect by about ten degrees from the heading she has been holding to for the past few hours. The course change will keep Jauhera at a greater minimum distance from the featherweed, but not by a substantial margin. Solveig gets the sense that what she is witnessing is the zep analogue of disdain; again, though, there's no way of really knowing. It's merely another data point, and she already has more of those than she knows what to do with.

Daycycle 60, pre-shift / WS-356.73R
It's visible on her lab-bench monitor, were she to peer in that direction, but she's conscientiously avoiding the distraction, focussing instead on

the task before her. Interfacing is not a skill that comes naturally to her, nor is it, seemingly, one which grows less difficult with repetition.

It is for Solveig a new day; the sun is readying itself to set. There's an orange-and-scarlet gleam dusting the upper haze layers, and an echo of this coloration finds its way somehow onto the white walls of the labspace. It's these hours, not the deep enduring night, nor the bright distended stretches of full daylight, that cause her body clock the greatest trouble, and for all that she has been on Rousseau for over four years now it is only these past few weeks in which the length of the planet's days has become a real problem for her. At the lake station, beneath the shroud of haze, the day's span was never an issue, the gradation between 'day' and 'dusk', or between 'dusk' and 'dark', scarcely worth observing. Here, though, aboard the *Wayfaring Stranger*, it's still disorienting to be faced with the setting of Rousseau's sun while knowing that her own day, her own period of activity has only recently begun anew. Her circadian rhythms are not thanking her.

Others, she's fairly sure, do not analogously suffer this perception of diurnal mixed messaging. She should ask someone how long it generally takes to acclimate. Ideally this should be someone who is not going to belittle or to find amusement in her question, and indeed she has someone in mind in this regard. But the work comes first.

She's working on the fourth featherweed platform—and struggling with the dual needs to ensure its operational functionality and to render its surface detailing sufficiently different to that of the other three which the zeps, apparently almost preternaturally adept at pattern-matching, will not have cause for heightened caution around the object and its siblings—when the call is relayed through the lab, at scarce more than a whisper. *Needlehawk.*

Solveig's instinctual reaction, confusion and unease, is more to do with the haste with which Bao and Torsten exit the labspace, headed for the ops deck, than with the word itself; that internal response comes through a second or two later, as cognition bites in.

There are several creatures known to prey on aging, ailing, immature or otherwise vulnerable zeps: lancegliders, danglers, kitescrapers, bladewings, even (in one chilling, grainily captured instance of which she's aware) the zep's own retinue of buoyancy-dependent remoras. But a full-grown zep free of any significant preexisting infirmity is an intrinsically hardy creature, and exceptionally difficult to kill. There is only one Rousseauvian creature considered capable of downing such a zep.

There's a needlehawk hunting, sufficiently close that the *Wayfaring Stranger*'s scopes have spied and flagged it. On the scale of the zeps themselves, and at the range the zeps keep from the *Wayfaring Stranger*, it seems a small thing, almost minuscule, a condor amidst blimps. A sharp-snouted dust mote.

The rules of biology are as inviolate as those of, say, physics; and yet their application is perhaps more varied. Rousseau's biochemistry is dramatically different to that of the terrestrial biosphere; and the upper atmosphere is not the veldt, nor the forest floor, nor the ocean's deeps. Here, altitude and gravity can combine to yield, on occasion, something not often encountered in other natural environments: the utter certainty of a delayed and brutally sudden death.

Solveig understands, well enough, the rushed activity of her colleagues. The needlehawk itself isn't necessarily of primary interest, although as an apex predator of sorts, infrequently sighted, it's sure to be closely monitored; rather, it's the implications of its ingress into zep airspace which have motivated the frenzy of researchers and technicians. The sled will need to be prepped and manned, ready to intercept whatever carcass the impending midair encounter throws down. It's a task in which she should be participating; but she can't.

She tells herself this isn't as much about any investment, on her part, in the zeps' wellbeing, as it is about the importance of remaining at her station. There will be things to learn in the minutes ahead. Encounters between zeps and needlehawks are by their nature high-altitude affairs and therefore seldom documented. Solveig is not at this moment aware of any which have occurred within a *congregation* of zeps. This is therefore an almost unprecedented opportunity to study the interaction, the communication, between the assembled zeps in a situation rife with the potential for crisis, pregnant with the possibility that an intelligent, communicative creature may lose its life. It's vital that she take best advantage of the opportunity.

It's more than merely vital. It's her *job*.

She runs through this argument in her mind, marshals it, polishes it, practises it for the near-certain recitation that will be required by her sceptical and antipathetic sci-section supervisor, all while Solveig commandeers and split-screens the labspace's largest display portal. She slaves the upper and lower left quadrants of the portal to the visuals from the two best-positioned featherweeds; the right-hand half of the screen provides the view from the *Wayfaring Stranger*'s scope, locked onto the still-distant needlehawk. Once the sled has launched, she'll run the feed from that onscreen in place of the ship's scope signal.

The scoped image, she's pleased to note, is a less-useful resolution than that provided by the nearest of her featherweeds, even if the cam-shake on her platforms is significantly more troublesome than is the judder from the airship's envelope-mounted scanners. Such defects can, after all, be smoothed out in the telemetry's post-processing.

There's a delay of a few seconds before the audio comes through. Overlaid on the static-swathed feed from the closest featherweed, she can hear the multi-voiced hubbub of the scientists and the tech workers clustered on the ops deck, all working to hasten the sled's launching. She damps the audio from her probes, double-checks that it is being recorded and saved, and amps the ops deck signal. She can discern the voices of Bao, Torsten, Sanna and Rewi, arguing over weight limits and equipment choice—therefore, over whatever is most likely to further their own research outcomes over those of their colleagues—while another voice (Isis, she thinks; one of the tech staff) is trying with fraying patience to explain to them all the trade-off that will be required between flight charge and launch time. (It seems a little surprising that the sled is not already fully charged and initialised, as it normally is, but Solveig gathers it has recently returned from an extended maintenance trawl over the upper reaches of the *Wayfaring Stranger*'s envelope.) Then her throat catches as she hears

Liam, reporting to those assembled that he has finished the vehicle's prop diagnostics and confirms it as ready to fly at their discretion. She's torn, now: wants to see Liam, who must be wondering why she isn't among those present amidst the ops deck's melee; but also needs to stay anchored to the labspace's viewscreen and to the controls for her featherweeds, so she can best monitor the danger to her zeps.

Her zeps. The thought's out there; she can't reel it back.

The possessiveness is understandable, she thinks—she has a lot invested, in an intellectual sense, in the sentients' wellbeing—but she knows full well that she has no genuine claim, no agency, over these fully-alien creatures. *Objectivity, Sol,* she tells herself. *Remember the taniwha, and the unjustified betrayal you felt at learning the truth of their life-cycle, just because you grew too deeply enmeshed in them. And the taniwha wanted to communicate with us, which is in sharp contradistinction to the zeps. Just let them be...*

Things happen fast. Onscreen, the needlehawk is within closing distance of the zep it's identified as its prey, and the zep's remoras have detached from their host in readiness for interception. Down on the ops deck, the sled's crew has been selected: Torsten and Liam.

Solveig winces at that; wants to be there, to wish Liam good fortune, to tell him she knows not what besides that. She's heard enough of the chatter of the past couple of minutes to know that the sled is to be launched only half-charged, so as to maximise the chance of getting close enough to intercept any casualties of the approaching dogfight: an intrinsically risky undertaking made more hazardous by hurried preparation. But she knows she wouldn't get down there in time to say anything to Liam, who's already suited and seated, nor to influence events in any useful capacity. All she can do is to watch and listen. It's a deeply dismaying feeling, sufficiently strong that she finds it difficult to concentrate on the screened imagery which is the primary reason for her isolation here, now, in the ship's deserted labspace.

The half-assembled featherweed sits reproachfully, forlorn, on her bench, like the abandoned remains of a meal half eaten. This, and some fugitive putrefaction-sharp odour from an imperfectly freeze-dried dangler tendril specimen in the supposedly sealed fumehood at her rear, are Solveig's only companions in the uncharacteristically empty environs of the lab.

The sled launches. It plummets disconcertingly before its props gain sufficient rotational traction to allow it to level out, then to slowly climb through the unbreathable air.

six

Daycycle 60, pre-shift / WS-356.73R

The needlehawk, sleek, broad-winged, long-tailed, buoyed only by the topmost remnants of the thermals in the airspace carpeting the haze-deck's vague upper surface, is moving near what's believed to be its operational ceiling of around eighteen kilometres. Flight in air this meagre is highly taxing; it has only a few minutes to make its kill. Even so, it's substantially better equipped for this than are the bulkier, stub-winged, partially buoyant remoras who must return and refasten themselves to their host zep within just a minute or so, or plunge with almost-certain finality to the surface.

If they're conscious of this peril, they don't display it. The remoras, Solveig sees, are harrying the needlehawk as a team, a pack: feinting and counter-feinting, seeking always to distract and to draw away the needlehawk from its target zep. There's a grace and an urgency both, she thinks, in the remoras' awkwardly wheeling flightpaths, as they strive by mass of numbers to impede the more agile predator's approach towards the zep. The sole factor in the half-dozen remoras' favour is that the cruelly sharp metre-long proboscis/ovipositor from which the needlehawk takes its name is an adaptation specifically optimised towards puncturing a zep's hide; while it can also inflict likely lethal damage to a heavier-than-air creature such as a remora, this danger comes at a serious cost. It is not unknown for the death throes of a needlehawk-impaled remora to result in the prey's adhesion surface latching fast upon the wing or torso of the predator, dooming the 'hawk via a gravitational imperative it is no longer aerodynamically equipped to resist. The needlehawk's attack behaviours, and its physiognomy, have doubtless evolved to minimise this hazard, just as the remoras' instincts are seemingly to place themselves in harm's way so as to coerce the needlehawk to abort the attack, or to doom itself should it grow too restless. But this zep's remoras are not, as yet, adopting such desperate protective measures: the flock's partially coordinated flight appears designed to steer the needlehawk away from its prey without any of the remoras coming within range of either its proboscis or its talons, which can as easily scythe through the dermis of a remora as they can anchor themselves within the hide of a zep. Perhaps the needlehawk knows that it need merely outwait its zep prey's defenders…

There's a shout from either Liam or Torsten—the latter, she thinks—as a remora succeeds in counterattack, diving down upon the needlehawk's mid-dorsal surface, and impacting solidly; the predator twists and struggles to regain steady flight while the remora performs an ungainly belly roll away from those raking claws. It and its fellow remoras now seem to be fleeing back to the dubious safety of their currently buoyant host.

What are they doing? Solveig wonders. *The needlehawk, at best, is only winded… they're giving up their lives more surely by reattaching themselves to the zep than by fighting on.* It's an unreasonable judgement on her part, she knows: these are creatures driven not by logic and by reasoning but by instinct. And yet surely the effect of evolution upon instinct is to hone it into a shape ideally adapted to promote survival, and therefore to mimic an optimised, even reasoned, course of action, in the face of repeatedly encountered threats? The remoras' retreat serves the needlehawk's intent, and its survival, better than it does their own; she cannot understand what she is seeing here.

Nor does she wish to see the zep, an unfathomable but sentient creature so much larger than a whale, slaughtered by a predator of scarcely human dimensions.

She is supposed to be a student of zep communication; she does not want to be a party to the communication of death. Her throat tightens as she reaches for the display screen's controls. She has never yet witnessed a sentient alien's death in real time; the idea horrifies her, somehow, more than the notion of human tragedy.

But seconds later, she sees that she has misread the situation. The beleaguered zep's remoras have seemingly all reattached themselves to their host; and yet the sky between needlehawk and zep is still busy with remoras. A dozen, perhaps more.

A chill runs the length of her back. This is behaviour which has never previously been documented. Another zep's remoras—in fact, more likely the full complement of two other zeps—have come to the aid of the harried entity. But there are no other zeps within the frame... Solveig zooms out and sees that the nearest zeps are fully two kilometres directly above the needlehawk's intended prey. In which case they are almost certainly safe themselves from this predator; but their remoras are unlikely to be able to climb far enough to reach their hosts once the needlehawk has been seen off.

It happens quickly. Three of the new remoras mob the needlehawk, fifty metres out from the zep's ship-broad flank. Within the melee, the needlehawk cavorts in desperation, striking one of the remoras with its talons and scraping such a broad gash through the creature's wing that its throes cascade into a helpless downward spiral. But in seeing off one harasser, the hunter of zeps has left its back exposed to the remaining two remoras, one of which noses in on the root of the needlehawk's right wing and yanks out a mouthful of musculature. The wing bends back as awkwardly as an inverted umbrella, and the needlehawk falls.

Several hundred metres below, Torsten and Liam make a snap judgment. They can intercept, at most, one of the two plummeting creatures.

They choose the remora.

The feed from the sled is harrowing, juddery and riven by the anguished wail of the doomed remora as it drops erratically through the sky. Torsten, seated at the sled's console, takes the shot; the first mesh-necked harpoon falls wide, but the second delivers the plunging remora a killing blow, striking it with sickening solidity behind the animal's broad, flat-topped head before the projectile's furled webbing erupts and ensnares the reflexively flailing creature. A third shot, already loosed before those in the sled can see that the missile before it has struck home, narrowly misses.

'Good shot,' is Liam's only comment.

Solveig feels her gorge rise. There's a difference between knowing that what the sled's occupants have done is, by some measure, humane—they have curtailed the needless suffering of a hapless, no longer flight-capable creature—and feeling in one's gut that the act she's just witnessed onscreen is something barbaric and shameful. *Zoology*, she thinks disgustedly. *At least xenolinguistics never kills anything in the name of progress.*

The sled sways alarmingly as the netted remora swings through the nadir of the cable by which it is now anchored to the craft, and for some seconds it does not appear that the crewed platform has sufficient motive power to check the descent the remora is dragging it towards. *Sever the cable*, Solveig pleads silently, not wishing to witness the impending disaster in which Liam seems sure to play a starring role; but the sled fights back against the planet's pull, slowly hauling itself upwards towards the safety of the *Wayfaring Stranger*'s ops deck.

The return takes minutes, and Solveig doesn't believe she's breathed once during the process.

For the next twelve hours, everyone on the science team cedes lab space to Torsten; or, more accurately, to the inflatable cleanroom that now dominates the labspace and into which the remora's carcass has been decanted for dissection. Solveig cannot but help view this operation with a blend of horror and fascination.

The remora does not quite fill the inflatable, the inflatable (pontooned across all three benches) does not quite fill the labspace, but its bulk does serve to make vivid the size of the creature in a manner which no amount of onscreen viewing and remote measurement can possibly emulate.

Torsten, his forearms deep within the thick-skinned waldoes through which he is leading the remora's inquisition-by-autoscalpel, has his back to the labspace's north wall; Rewi and Sanna, assisting him on the opposite side of the inflatable, are similar pressed against the south wall, within earshot but out of direct line of sight of both Torsten and Solveig, who has sequestered herself in the corner adjacent to the labspace's door. She's resigned herself to a lack of further progress on the featherweed for today.

She wishes to watch, but she's not comfortable with this form of science's physicality. She may need the escape route, whatever Hong might think of her for choosing it.

The remora's wing is a mess: almost tattered, the rents in its grey down-fuzzed membrane edged in the ink-black blood that already mats the inflatable's pontoon-supported base. From here she cannot see the damage wrought by the harpoon's head—the creature has been laid on its back, for greater access to its sensory organs, digestive tract, and genitals—but she doubts that such a vista would be more unsettling than the sightless, lidless stare of its pallid, tripartite-pupilled eye.

Torsten is working fast: though decomposition of the intrinsically soft-tissued creatures of Rousseau's upper atmosphere is no quicker than the terrestrial process, and by some measures might be considered to be somewhat slower, the largely sedentary remoras are generally host to a plethora of diminutive parasites which, no longer held in check by the creature's metabolic defences, are certain to be seizing the remora's demise as an opportunity to feed and to reproduce. The widely shared joke among xenobiologists is that a creature dead at this altitude will be consumed to dust before it impacts with the planet's surface; it's an exaggeration, of course, but in the way of such things it's pearled around a grain of truth.

Daycycle 60, shift 2 / WS-356.76R
Outside, as the sun-warmed air fades through twilight, something quietly remarkable is occurring. It's not directly perceived by any among the *Wayfaring Stranger*'s science crew, but it's fortuitously captured by

the directed surveillance from two of Solveig's featherweeds. It will go undetected for the best part of a Rousseauvian day before Solveig, her mind predominantly on other matters, is able to satisfactorily breach the lengthening backlog of observations, and it will not be properly understood for quite some time beyond that.

It is almost as though the zeps, at distances from the airship of generally more than six kilometres, have consciously opted to wait until such time as the researchers' attention is fully occupied elsewhere.

Daycycle 60, shift 2 / WS-356.77R

How did Rousseau's life originate? There's a hypothesis which, in the way of such things, would appear to be almost irredeemably unverifiable— for the planet's fossil record, particularly of the aerobiota, is intrinsically sparse and difficult to properly characterise—but which to Solveig's mind sounds at least as plausible as any of its competitors. This hypothesis proposes that, just as the first blush of Earthlife may well have ensued on the thermally steep and chemically intriguing fringes of submarine hydrothermal vents, so too might Rousseau's flirtation with protobiology have first occurred within regions of significant temperature gradient and highly promising chemical complexity: the haze deck. The planet's lowest and most nearly opaque sheath of haze is warmed atop by scarcely filtered sunlight and underlaid by a refrigerated twilight courtesy of the great variety of light-absorbing organic molecules—some chemically inert, some highly reactive—amassed there, susceptible to molecular transactions such as modification, unsaturation, polymerisation, and condensation. The haze layer, in short, is host on an abiotic level to those very processes on which Rousseauvian life depends; and naturally enough it is also host to a diversity of lifeforms seeking to exploit every niche within its untidily layered structure. Might one cohort of those lifeforms constitute a kind of living fossil, a more-or-less-faithful representation of a creature truly ancestral to all other organisms on Rousseau? Solveig doesn't know, cannot know, need not really concern herself with such notions: she's a xenolinguist, not an exobiologist, though of course she has some training in both terrestrial and Rousseauvian biology, and she necessarily has some layperson's interest in these ideas.

It's because of this interest that, watching Torsten's pitiless structural inquisition of the remora carcass, she now makes an unexpected connection. The bodyform of the remora—a creature which, so far as she knows, never ventures in life beneath the lower fringes of the haze-deck, and which for its full adult life clings fast to the side or underside of a zep several kilometres above that haze-deck—is a disorientingly close match to that of an entity found only within the chill, dark depths of Rousseau's hydrocarbon lakes and seas. The adult form of the taniwha.

The recognition is unsettling, and she's not sure what to do with it. The similarity is not so striking that any person would ever mistake one for the other: on an anatomical level, there must be significant differences between a creature adapted to the cold and pressure of deep immersion, and one making as many concessions to flight as its size and appetite permit. The remora is larger, less streamlined, bloated with an internal air bladder that is more probably an adaptation designed for vocalisation than for any pretence towards buoyancy, sheathed in a fuzz that seems, amongst the creatures of Rousseau's atmosphere, to be the closest approximation towards feathers that has yet been manifested here; the adult taniwha is denser, possessing a thick layer of thermally insulating musculature, and with a swim bladder in approximately the same place as the remora's gas reservoir. There are obvious differences, too, in the shape of the limbs, but the body, the head, the placement of the eyes, the location of the limbs along the side of the body: there's no reason Solveig can advance for why these aspects should be so similar in two essentially unrelated creatures adapted to very different environments, leading to the suggestion that they may indeed be, in a phylogenetic sense, cousins or something yet closer.

The taniwha pass through a sentient phase. The remoras adhere to sentients. The two resemble each other. Does it mean anything? How can it, across a vertical score of kilometres?

The nausea surges without anything in the way of bodily premonition. She barely makes it to the labspace's slow-opening door before the first regurgitative swell sours her throat. She hurries to the closest restroom, bends over a basin flecked with sanitiser and dried mouthrinse, and expels what remains of her two most recent meals. She waits until she's sure the episode has concluded before pushing herself back properly upright, eyes dampened, limbs drained of energy. She wipes her mouth on her sleeve, checks her clothing, runs a little water into the basin, cups her hands beneath the spigot, rinses her mouth cautiously. Eyes without favour the paled, draggle-haired creature she sees in the mirror.

<Are you alright?> the restroom inquires: soothing; patient; concerned.

'I'm fine,' she replies.

<Do you require medical attention?>

'No.'

<Would a shower help?>

'I'm *fine*,' she repeats. Leaves the restroom before it can pry further.

Wonders, in the corridor, where she should go. Not back to the lab. Nor to her room.

There really aren't that many choices of venue in a research airship gondola.

Daycycle 60, shift 2 / WS-356.77R

The rec lounge is free for only a few minutes before her solitude is interrupted. But as fate would have it, the interruption is welcome enough. The whole time she's been here, carefully seated with her back to the vista of Rousseau's busily inhabited upper atmosphere, her head has been spinning.

She can't decide whether she feels irked or relieved that Liam hasn't noticed—or at least hasn't remarked upon—the peakiness she's sure she must be conveying. Nor is she certain whether it's wholeheartedly sensible to be introducing coffee into a stomach so peremptorily and recently purged, but she needs the sense of normality that coffee conveys.

Liam is relating his afternoon to her, his excursion in the sled now sufficiently an episode of ancient history that it doesn't require comment. Instead, what she gets is an explanation centring on a difference of opinion between himself, and Isis, and Cordero regarding the importance of a bracket of apparently malfunctioning sensors imprinted within the fabric of the envelope. It takes her a few minutes to recognise that his repeated references to degrees of latitude and longitude, and of the various compass points, are not descriptions of planetary location but rather of placement upon the *Wayfaring Stranger*'s strongly prolate fuselage, with 'North' representing the zenith, 'South' the nadir (and the gondola), and an elliptical equator encompassing one hundred and eighty degrees each of East and West. This realisation made, she berates him good-naturedly about the illogicality of such a counterintuitive system of reference; as conversational gambits go, it doesn't lead anywhere directly, but it serves to break the thread of his reiteration of his afternoon's work.

She pours something of herself into the breach.

'I had to bail out on the dissection just now,' she tells him. It feels like a confession, and in a sense it is: researchers are supposed to be accustomed to such things.

'I can understand that,' he responds, his tone suggesting concern. 'It can be unsettling seeing all those viscera.'

'It wasn't that,' she says. 'It was… it was more because of something I noticed, once the dissection got underway. Liam, it felt wrong.'

'Wrong why? The remora was as good as dead. It wasn't flight-capable, it couldn't even make it back to its host; if anything, it was—'

'A kindness. Yes, I know that argument. And I don't disagree with that per se. And I know we need to be able to source specimens for anatomical study, and to be able to do so in an ethical manner. I accept all of that… but it still feels wrong. I mean, we didn't obtain consent.'

'From the zep? That was never an option, in the moment, even if we did know how to communicate with them. Are you trying to make out that this is some kind of failing on your part, to initiate contact with them?'

'No. I mean, no I don't mean that it's my failing, and no, I wasn't referring to the zeps.'

'Then I don't understand what you mean by consent, in this situation.'

'The remora. Liam, I think they're intelligent.'

He smiles slightly, studies her face. The smile subsides. 'You're serious.'

'I'm… I'm not sure,' she replies. Meets his gaze. 'Yes, I'm serious. But at this stage it's nothing more than a hunch, hardly even that really. I don't have any evidence to support it, well nothing I can really point to; it's not even my place to amass such evidence, and I don't think I would know where to start. I just knew I couldn't stay watching the dissection. The autopsy.'

'I can see that,' he says, his glance sliding away towards her left. 'I think.'

'I don't see why. I haven't explained it at all well. I doubt that I even can explain it.' She looks down at her upturned hands, suddenly it seems fascinated by the whorls of her fingertips. 'I probably shouldn't have mentioned it; but I think I needed to hear myself say it, to find out exactly how crazy an idea it sounded, and you were here. And I feel I can talk to you safely about these things.'

'Do you think it sounds crazy?' he asks her.

'Do you?' she feints back.

'I asked you first. And I wouldn't know one way or another. You're the one qualified in such things.'

She stares at him, almost to the point of rudeness. 'No,' she offers, eventually. 'No, I don't think it sounds crazy. Well, not entirely.'

'There you go, then.' He stands. 'I'd love to stay and talk, Doc, but I'd better get back to ensuring Isis and Cordero don't mess up at the controls.'

'Of course,' she says. 'I should be getting back too. I'd probably better watch the rest of it.'

'You'll be okay?'

'I think so.' She pauses. 'But can I ask you a favour?'

'What would that be?'

'Please don't say anything about this... crazy idea of mine. I don't think it would increase my stock among the science crew.'

'Discretion is my watchword.' He smiles. 'I really do have to go.'

'Of course. Thank you, Liam.'

'No problem, Doc.'

She watches him go, then stares into her coffee mug as though it might hold the answer to any of her questions. It doesn't.

She heads back towards the lab.

No, it's not a crazy idea, not entirely. But that doesn't mean it's necessarily right.

seven

Daycycle 61, early / WS-356.88R

It's a variant on a dream she's had before: the bodysuit, the taniwha, the sense of something significant and private. She wakes, heartrate elevated, breathing shallow. Is momentarily disoriented by the near-darkness of her cabin: for the dream, on this occasion, placed itself not in the cold and pressing lightlessness of the taniwhas' crater lake, but in the limitless brilliance of Rousseau's upper atmosphere.

What does it say about me, she wonders, *that my subconscious equates communication with physical interaction?*

And why am I having thoughts of skinsuits in connection with the remoras?

But what would it mean if...

Her breath catches as the dream's fanciful sequelae cascade through her still sleep-stunned mind. She knows the dangers of this mode of thinking: ideas which appear, at first flush, to have the edge of perfection, the freight of import, the burst of novelty, may well, within minutes, reveal themselves to be merely mundane, misinformed, disappointing. She gives herself up to the speculation nonetheless.

Zeps are self-aware, numerate. Taniwha, at least in their immature form, are self-aware, articulate, social, communicating through touch. Remoras spend their adult lives clinging to the hide of a large sentient animal. If the taniwhas' aerial lookalikes share not only their acquisition of sentience but also their intricately haptic mode of expression, might not each remora be involved in a near-continual dialogue with the creature that provides it with the security of buoyancy-by-proxy?

The implication, innately unprovable, is sufficiently startling that for an instant she is not sure of her balance, as though she is as unaccustomed to the gondola's oscillations as when she first came aboard those several weeks ago. *We've been thinking of the zeps, all along, as though they're aloof aerial leviathans, who make no display of curiosity towards us because they're solitary beings with no need for contact. Hermits, more or less. But what if they are simply too constantly busy communicating with their attendants to be bothered with us?*

What if, like the taniwha, they too communicate through their dermis?

The scientific method: put it up, then challenge it.

Since she cannot, as yet, entrust such a counterintuitive or unorthodox proposal to any of her colleagues, the devil's advocacy it requires needs therefore to be her own.

We know that zeps communicate over significant distances by vocalisation and by chameleonism, and perhaps through other techniques. There's no need to invoke any kind of concealed or private communication, on their part, with creatures that aren't currently known to be intelligent. It's not the simplest solution to the problem of the remoras' morphological similarity to the taniwha. It doesn't explain anything. Let it go.

But if it were true...

If it were true, then we might not need to resolve the zeps' long-distance communication modes, in order to speak with them. We might be able to make contact... by making contact. With a skinsuit, or a remote-signalled waldo. Like we did with the taniwha.

Of course the catch is that, even if it does exist, we know nothing of the remoras' body language. And we've no conceivable way of learning it. Even if it does exist.

Now get yourself to the lab, and do some actual work.

She shrugs, sorts clothing for the day ahead, dresses. Prepares herself mentally to negotiate breakfast in the rec lounge, to face colleagues in the lab. And to keep crazy ideas to herself.

The sight of the maintenance drone heedlessly defying gravity's pull as it scrapes clean—or at least cleaner—the outer surface of the rec lounge's viewscreen doesn't help her in this resolve.

Daycycle 65, shift 2 / WS-357.78R

The ambition stays with her, for all that she knows it would be a wasted effort to request the resources for some kind of sensory-glove remora mimic, whether suit or waldo. Hong would never approve it, either on the grounds of material-expenditure, mission profile, or researcher safety; and there is an innate policy of cautiousness regarding zep studies that the remora-suit concept would flout. The initiation of contact with the zeps is, of course, something treated as a priority amongst the research community (hence Solveig's presence on the *Wayfaring Stranger*), but it must come about in a carefully incremental manner, which presents her with a dilemma: if she wishes to have longevity among the *Stranger's* research complement, she will need to show definite and significant progress in her project, without attempting anything that contravenes the broader research spirit of prudence and patient incrementality. The last thing she needs is to be pursuing something seen as a fringe hypothesis, some rationale for which she is the sole adherent: while science often requires the overturning or challenging of cherished but flawed concepts, scientists are still, in some important senses, herd creatures.

It's Torsten who ultimately provides her with the 'in' she requires; he does so quite inadvertently (for he is as ignorant of Solveig's ponderings as is anyone else amongst the *Wayfaring Stranger's* scientists) and through the distinctly unprepossessing medium of the research presentation. Her own attendance at the presentation is in turn almost equally inadvertent: while science naturally interests her, particularly when it concerns the biology of Rousseau, the glacial and pedantic narrations of scientific endeavour that are captured within any soliloquistic presentation have long been capable only of inducing torpor in her, and her policy has accordingly been to spare her colleagues the sight of her sedentarily sleeping form at any of these events. But the regular meeting room is unavailable, and Torsten's presentation is relocated to the rec lounge...

Arrogant, she thinks, watching him preparing to start. *The self-confidence of the young, the tall, the never-yet-thwarted, the surefootedness of someone sufficiently gifted with luck to have had an easy route into a promising field of investigation...* and chides herself for her defensiveness. *When did you become such a curmudgeon, Sol?*

But if self-commentary is the strategy which Solveig has adopted so as to maintain wakefulness under conditions hardly conducive to its sustenance, such considerations swiftly dissipate with Torsten's first sentences, which catch her categorically unawares. For the next several minutes she's stunned, effectively adrift, almost bewildered by the conceptual disruption initiated by her colleague's analysis. She knows too little of the detail of the Rousseauvian biomolecular machinery that occupies an analogous role to that filled, in terrestrial organisms, by DNA or by RNA, but she knows that others in this small audience are as well-versed in the subject as anyone yet living, and if they are sitting silently and without significant protest then it follows that there are no crippling flaws in what Torsten is describing. She thinks, at first, that what he is describing is essentially what she has been too timorous to propose, that he has stumbled on her secret hypothesis of remora sentience through independent endeavour, but it is not this. It's something yet more bizarre, more unexpected. And it's all the covering fire Solveig could ever require.

They don't see the deeper implications, she thinks, listening as the others question Torsten over his methods, his observations, his conclusions, and as he responds with details of supporting evidence and instrumental calibration she can only fumblingly follow, nonspecialist in this field that she is. But there's more to it than even Torsten realises. *They're all so caught up in the biological novelty of it that they're oblivious to what it means in a cultural sense, what it tells us about zep society. There is nothing like this in all of vertebrate biology, nothing in all of human interaction. How do we talk to a beehive, to a tree, to a coral outcrop? What must it be like to live like that?*

How can we start to show that we have the potential to understand their way of being?

What can I say to them, to convince them, to interest them in us, when I know neither their tongue nor their mindset?

Are they even knowable, in a human sense?

The gathering breaks up. Solveig is slow to return to the labspace; when she does, she fails to achieve anything of value, can hardly keep up even with checking that the featherweeds are keeping any zeps in their respective fields of view. Her mind is too busy for such things.

Daycycle 65, end of shift 2 / WS-357.82R

She needs to talk these things over. Needs to hear whether her interpretation is crazy, improbable, or just sufficiently odd to be true. And there's only one person she trusts sufficiently, among the twenty-odd individuals who populate the *Wayfaring Stranger*, to unburden herself on these matters. (And why is it, though, that this condition has come to pass? She casts her mind back, but can't truly be sure.)

It's difficult to see, nonetheless, how to raise it in conversation: she's no wish to be bludgeoning him with her wild hypotheses.

As it happens, he brings the subject up himself, or near enough. Torsten's revelation has apparently propagated through the vessel like fire or a gas leak. Liam has heard it from Isis, who heard it from someone else at tech-shift changeover…

'Is it true?' he asks, before he's taken so much as a mouthful. 'That the remoras are zeps too?'

'It's…' She makes a false start on her reply: throat too dry, delivery indistinct. Retries, aiming for just sufficient clarity that her words won't propagate past him. It's difficult to have a private conversation in the rec lounge. (Not that science should be private, but she's not on solid ground here.) 'It's not quite that simple. They're different creatures, different forms. But the remora that Torsten studied had all the same paragenetic material that our few available samples of zep tissue also have, just expressed differently.'

'What does that mean?'

'Torsten and the others are still arguing it back and forth. At first I think he thought they were simple gender differences—like the remora is the male form, the zep the female, but it's more complicated. The remoras are technically hermaphroditic, in the sense of having all the paragenetic material needed to adopt characteristics of either gender—that is, if we know enough about the sexual expression of Rousseau's animal life. Torsten has a theory that the remoras aren't produced through sexual reproduction, but through budding—they're genetically the same as their parent zep, but they develop remnant male and/or female characteristics as they mature, perhaps under the influence of hormones, or their equivalent, which are produced by the zep. Torsten said the specimen they dissected did not appear to have genuine reproductive capability, I didn't follow what his evidence was for that, but it's one of the reasons he advances for a budding hypothesis. He calls them 'client organisms'— they'd be incapable of any sort of separate existence at this altitude, they're more or less fully dependent on the zep, but they obviously fulfil a role in keeping their host safe. But they're so caught up in the biological novelty of it that they can't see the ramif—'

'When you say 'they', there, that last bit, you mean you lot? The science complement?'

'Yes. They're trying to map it in terrestrial biology terms, as though it's queens and workers, or something similar. But it can't be anything like that. Liam, they don't know what they've got.'

'What have they got?'

'We've been viewing the zeps as loners. Inflatable hermits. But they're not that at all. They're each one a community. And it makes sense of this congregating behaviour—it's not just birthing that has brought them together. They're looking to trade off remoras with each other. Looking for mates. Like flowers striving to avoid self-pollination. That's the biological argument, I'm sure Torsten has already mapped that out, at least as a possibility, but I reckon there are levels he hasn't twigged to.'

'Is this your remoras-are-intelligent-too idea?'

'Well, yes,' says Solveig, 'but I don't think I'd explained to you just why I had that thought. It's'—she looks around the rec lounge, carefully not catching anyone's eye—'probably better discussed in private.' She stands. 'Care to tag along?'

'This a short walk or a long walk?' Liam asks.

'Short.'

'You don't have to ask twice,' he says, rising from the couch.

Daycycle 65, postshift / WS-357.85R

'So zeps are sentient.' Solveig is seated cross-legged on her sleeping surface, counting items off on her fingers.

'With you so far,' says Liam. He's lying half-on, half-off the sleeping surface. _Like some form of marine mammal,_ she thinks, allowing a quick smile at the notion. A walrus, maybe, leaning on his arms like that. It doesn't look comfortable, but she decides there's space enough that he could straightforwardly adopt a sitting posture at that end of the sleeping surface if he so chose.

'Meaning they have ideation, individuation, complex communication, some grasp of symbolic logic—'

'Wait. How do we know all this? They won't talk to us.'

'Mostly, it flows from numeracy,' she explains. A tress of hair dislodges itself from behind her ear as she's speaking; she reaches back with her hand to curl it back into place. 'We've eavesdropped on them counting in hexadecimal. That's from one of the earliest observations, made years ago, it's one of our foundational items of evidence of sentience. I mean, that still only gives us a very bare-bones understanding of what their sentience might be like, but it's generally accepted that those, at least, are fairly safe assumptions. We're a long way, as yet, from a proper zep-centred theory of mind.'

'Okay.'

'Remoras are probably also sentient.'

'Go on.'

Solveig appreciates that he seems to be keeping up with her. He's not trained in her field; but he's smart, and he appears to make mental connections quickly. She unfolds a third finger. 'Taniwha are sentient. We've built up quite a good map of taniwha sentience space, through our efforts at contact with them. It doesn't bear much similarity to anything terrestrial, but it's a coherent and quite appealing way of communicating.' She finds herself struggling in the attempt to suppress a blush. 'They're not so big on individuation, heavy on metaphor. Quite playful in their way. Short attention span, though. It can be very difficult to get them to stay on topic.'

'Are you only bringing taniwha into this because you're familiar with them?'

'Not exactly. Four—and this is the connection I don't think Torsten or the others will twig to, because they have that upper-atmosphere science mindset that shows no interest in anything that happens beneath the haze. Point four: remoras are ringers for taniwha.'

'Are they? I wouldn't have said—'

'They are. There are differences, but they're quite superficial. But I think most peoples' ideas of the taniwha come from that series of artworks— we don't have direct visual images, and the radar and sonar tomography images don't really give a clear impression. There are probably only a dozen people on the planet who have a reliable image of what the taniwha look like, and those are the linguists and the technicians who've worked on those projects.' She sees herself back in the lab, carefully running the hand on a full-body waldo down the stippled flank of Blue Six...

'Aren't taniwha... kind of blubbery?' Liam asks.

'I wouldn't have said that. Their skin's adapted to the conditions deep within the liquid environment, so in that sense it's different from a remora's, yes, but their anatomies are startlingly similar. I think they're closely related. Which bolsters the case for remora sentience.'

He pulls himself to his feet, flexes his shoulders, takes a seat on the sleeping surface. 'So does that mean taniwha are somehow related to zeps too? If zeps and remoras are basically two forms of the same thing?'

'I think it must,' says Solveig.

'Okay, so what now?'

'Nothing now.'

'But there must be some way you can use this. I mean, if you can talk to taniwha and it turns out that taniwha and zeps are quite closely related—wait, does this mean that if you know the taniwha language, you already know how to talk to zeps?'

'I doubt it. First of all, there's no such thing as 'the taniwha language'. There are several populations of taniwha, in the large lakes and seas; so far as we can tell, they've been isolated from each other for ages. I learnt how to speak with one population, in one lake; but I'd be starting almost from scratch in trying to establish communication with a different population. With zeps it'd be like, I guess, thinking I could communicate with orang-utans just because I knew English and French. It'd be more problematic than that, because at least among the great apes there are some commonalities of body language. But the taniwha communication is *all* body language, and it differs from lake to lake. So I wouldn't know where to start, and my preconceptions would probably be more trouble than help.'

'Still—'

She sighs. 'Liam, you need to remember, this is all just my supposition. Just my brain seeing a connection that may well not be founded in reality. There's no proof. And I don't see how to get any, short of encountering a zep willing to participate in communication.'

'But can't you just, you know, float the idea? Write it up or something?'

'It doesn't work that way. I'd need evidence. And with my history in taniwha studies, people would write it off as a gimmicky attempt to buy in on zeps. I don't have a track record in upper-atmosphere biology, nor in anatomy. I'd need both of those, and I have neither.'

'Could you collaborate with someone who does? That's something you lot do, isn't it?'

'It'd have to be Torsten,' says Solveig. 'He's the one with the remora credentials. But aside from the fact that we don't have any evidence—'

'There must be tissue samples of taniwha, wouldn't there be?' Liam asks. 'Because then you can compare them with the remora—'

'That's actually a good idea. But the catch is, it's a xenogenetic approach.'

'A what?'

'Torsten's speciality. I'd need evidence through a comparative linguistic approach. That's the only way it would be seen as my research, and not Torsten's.'

'Does that matter so much?'

'It pretty much does,' replies Solveig, hoping he doesn't ask *why*. Because she's not at all sure why. She shakes her head, shuffles closer to where Liam is awkwardly balanced on the sleeping surface's edge. 'Actually, something I was thinking yesterday…'

'Yes?'

'It's a language based on touch. Taniwha, I mean. It's— I don't know, it's hard to describe it to someone. It's subtle. And very expressive.' She holds her hand up, palm outward, a short distance from Liam's chest. 'I've wondered, ever since I first met the taniwha, what it must be like to have that as your primary sense, primary form of communication. They're blind and mute. They have some hearing, and taste I guess, but mostly it's touch. It's maybe like having implants.'

He looks up from her hand to her face, presses his palm against hers. 'Implants are mainly confusing, to start with. Then you get used to them. I wouldn't say they're anything special, they just become part of you.'

'But they give you abilities that most other people don't have.'

'Well, sure. For my job. I mean, they help to diagnose equipment.'

'What's that like?'

'It's work. It's, I don't know, it helps.'

She pulls her hand back, extends her arm to grab his hand at the wrist. Gently moves it to her shoulder. 'Diagnose *me*,' she says.

So he does.

Daycycle 66, early / WS-357.89R
What I need, she tells herself, *is an outfit that suggests a remora-like capacity for tactile communication without overtly seeming to mimic the appearance*

of a remora. Because it's essential I don't provoke a suspicion that the approach is a disguised attack.

But I have no way of knowing what, to a zep, would count as a disguise.

It's still deep darkness, of course: the length of the Rousseauvian night sees to that. She has the sense, though, that she's managed only two or three hours of sleep. She should be seeking more, but her mind has sprung into activity with a freewheeling productive clarity that she desperately hopes is not illusory. The notion of sleep isn't aided, either, by the radiant heat of Liam lying beside her, sporadically murmuring words she cannot quite hear but which she's sure are not in any waking language.

It would be selfish to wake him.

She nestles against his warmth, her mind moving in what seems a hundred disparate directions.

It's best kept simple, she decides. *A standard skysuit, no camo, augmented perhaps with upsized sensepads on the gloves… the fewer adornments, the fewer aspects that can be interpreted as attempts to disguise or deceive.*

She allows herself to envisage the adapted skysuit, to feel the flush of accomplishment. She plans it out. Within the compact limits of her cabin, Liam warm and asleep beside her, the quiet darkness: it's all straightforward. There is no need to complicate matters. She will just do this. She *can* do this.

She drifts back asleep believing this.

eight

Daycycle 68, start of shift / WS-358.31R

She rises later, this daycycle, than she has intended to, hastily disentangles herself from Liam, apologises, savours one last time his lips' taste, hurries to the lab. There are several actions that should, instead, take priority—breakfast, a wash, fresh clothing—but she has no time, right now, for such mundane human considerations. The monitors beckon. Plus it's getting loud outside, a chorus of low booming tones, chittering with structure and just on the threshold of human perception, and she's reasonably sure she knows what that means.

She's the first one in to the lab. Even so, she's too late; it's already happened. She can hear, can see, that a part of the incident has been captured, peripherally, on playback, but that's no sop to her disappointment. There will be other opportunities—or so she hopes—to monitor the birthing process, but it's not possible to know how much time she has to play with. And she needs to get that sixth featherweed out there, to maximise her chances of documenting the event.

But first—she stretches the fabric of her shopworn tunic's armpit, sniffs—she very much needs to freshen. And to eat.

Rewi and Sanna are at their respective stations when she returns to the lab, twenty minutes later; she has the feeling she's interrupted something.

But she can't be bothered investing any speculative energy on the private lives of her colleagues, and focuses on task as sternly as though she were equipped with blinkers. So immersed is she in completing the sixth featherweed's assembly that she almost misses the second birth, occurring not more than a kilometre from her eye-in-the-sky; growing aware of a renewed burst of zepsong from several directions at once, she only just catches a peripheral hint of the languid zep barrel-roll that initiates the process. The assembly can wait; all her attention is now directed to the monitors, and to her communication with the active obs platform. It's delicate: she needs to elevate the featherweed, which has lost some buoyancy during the night, but she also very much needs not to spook the mother-to-be. (For her own purposes, the audio will be the crucial component, but she'll need the accompanying visual record to be as informative as possible, so as to provide the clearest and most direct context for the still-indecipherable snippets of zep communication. And she may be mistaken, but she doesn't think anyone else has yet managed to document a zep birth on audio, close-up …)

Daycycle 68, shift 1 / WS-358.35R
At first it looks like nothing more than a blister, a slightly darkened bump at the top of the zep's tawny hide, tiny compared to its mother's immensity. It protrudes reasonably rapidly, becomes a shaded, translucent cupola, at perhaps a half-metre across still minuscule against its parent's bulk. There's a pause, while from several directions the zepsong continues deafeningly, then within a few further seconds the birth is complete, with the infant zep pushed fully out into the world. It is, Solveig thinks, somewhat anticlimactic: the newborn zep is much smaller than she had been expecting, not much more than fifty or sixty centimetres in diameter, and it's just lodged there, anchored somehow still to its mother. *Isn't it supposed to rise free? Isn't that the dual purpose of the host of zeps riding a few kilometres above the birthing flock, not just to generate sufficient noise to repel the numerous predators that would otherwise gather to capitalise on the*

opportunities for plunder, but also to act as guardians to the neonates on their first and most hazardous voyage into the sky?

Why doesn't it float free? Has something gone wrong?

But then something unexpected happens. The infant starts to swell. At first Solveig doesn't believe the process she's witnessing, preferring instead to presume that she'd merely misjudged the newborn's initial diameter, but after a couple of minutes it's undeniable that the creature has visibly grown, and continues to grow. A few minutes more, and it rises slightly away from its mother's hide, tethered by a short umbilicus of perhaps ten centimetres' width.

'That's impressive,' remarks Rewi, standing behind Solveig's shoulder. 'I didn't know they did that.'

'I don't think anybody knew they did that,' says Solveig, with a sense of accomplishment she cannot entirely suppress.

'Stands to reason, though,' says Sanna, who has also crowded in to watch. (*Great*, thinks Solveig. *An entourage.*) 'I mean, as an adaptation to make birth less traumatic. Zeps are mainly gaseous, so they can just inflate after birth.'

'I don't see how that would be less traumatic,' says Rewi.

'I'm thinking from the *mother's* perspective, Rewi,' replies Sanna, with enough of an edge to suggest that there's some history between these two. Then her voice softens. 'So this is from that platform you launched yesterday?'

'Yes,' says Solveig, bristling at the others' chatter but, in view of her perceived position within the lab's unspoken hierarchy, not feeling able to give full voice to her indignation. *But some peace and quiet so I could try to tease out the zepsong's syntax doesn't seem too much to ask.*

'I don't suppose you have any mass spec capability on that platform?' asks Sanna.

'No,' Solveig responds. 'I always struggle meeting buoyancy with them as it is.'

'Pity,' says Sanna. 'I'd bet there's some full-on chemical signalling going on with all that.'

There may well be, Solveig remarks to herself. 'It's the audio I'm interested in.'

'Have I missed something?' Bao asks from the lab's doorway.

Daycycle 68, shift 2 / WS-358.39R

The novelty wears off; the audience dissipates as the morning segues into afternoon. Three more births occur over the span of a few hours; Solveig wishes, now, that she had persevered with completing the sixth featherweed's construction, because the existing ones are badly overtaxed trying to shuttle between birth sites several kilometres apart. She does not get as good a record of any of the subsequent events as she believes she has obtained of the first (though she knows she will need to listen to that one anew, to seek to elucidate alien meaning without the cluttered interference of background human chatter). One of the additional events appears to be a close copy of the first incident; one is a multiple birth, producing three smaller and slower-to-rise infant zeps; one is a stillborn, that neither inflates nor breaks free from the umbilicus. She chooses to call it a day rather than witness the fate of that small, lifeless globe.

Daycycle 68, late / WS-358.44R

She knows who it is before she slides the door apart—nobody else is so palpably accompanied by an intense sweet-sharp perfume aura—but what she can't imagine is *why* Bao might be visiting her in her cabin.

'Hi,' she says, after a pause just long enough to offer them an unclaimed opportunity to speak first.

Bao returns the monosyllable.

'Is something up?' Solveig asks, hoping it isn't. Her mouth's dry. Her head's still sore around the edges.

'No,' says Bao. Hesitates. 'May I come in?'

'Of course.' It takes her a few seconds to step aside from the doorway. Maybe it's the migraine's aftermath, maybe it's simple embarrassment.

She's conscious her quarters are messy, clothing and bedding in disarray: housekeeping holds no attraction for her, and she hasn't been expecting company. She moves a few garments further across her sleeping surface, sits down, glances up at Bao. The slender little botanist's face does not look entirely at ease. *That makes two of us*, she thinks. She refuses to feel guilt at the mess, though this effort's not wholly successful. *It would be easier if I'd been doing something constructive with my time.*

'You're probably aware I've been delegated with collating this quarter's research report,' they say. Their tone's a poor carrier of enthusiasm.

'Yes.' Actually, Solveig hasn't known this; or if she has, she's forgotten it. 'Take a seat.'

There's only the sleeping surface; Bao remains standing. 'I'm required to collect summaries from each of the research contingent. Yourself included.'

'Of course,' says Solveig, pausing to take a long sip from her water bulb. She shuffles across, still seated, so as to lean herself against the cabin wall, to give Bao more space to sit. 'But if that's all this is about, isn't this something which could be more straightforwardly discussed during lab time?'

'Indeed,' Bao responds. 'But… might I ask you to seal the door?'

Solveig's puzzled by their request, but Bao's no threat. She arranges the door's closure. Waits.

'The summaries are an important metric of research progress by each individual or group aboard the *Wayfaring Stranger*. They're used to assess grounds for continuity… or severance… of each project.' The words sound carefully chosen, practised. Rehearsed.

'Are you saying you don't think I've achieved enough onboard?' Solveig replies, surprised at the level of irritation that's been sparked within her by Bao's oblique phrasing and delivery. 'I'd hardly say that was your place to be judging me on that.'

'It's not.' They pause. It's obvious they're not comfortable with some part of this. They open their mouth to say something that stays unsaid, cough quietly as though that had been their intention. 'The decision on such matters is made… at a higher level.'

'You're telling me Hong wants me gone?'

Again, the response is delayed. 'I'm not fully apprised of such details,' says Bao, frowning. 'And if I were, I would not be in a position to be passing such on.' They pause once more. 'But I think there is a mood on the vessel, among certain quarters, for… replacement.'

'Whose mood?' Solveig asks, wondering if the rancidity in her mouth is another migraine after-effect, or something else.

Bao splays their hands outwards. 'None of us,' they say. 'It is because I would want to see you stay on here that I'm apprising you of my suspicions.'

'Why should you want me to stay on?' she asks, creasing her brow. 'My research has nothing to do with yours, nor Sanna's, nor Rewi's, and only has some short-lived accidental overlap with Torsten because of the remora dissection and the findings that've come out of that. So—'

'We think what you're doing is important,' Bao says. 'You're a valuable member of the team. And you're well-liked.'

I don't see why, she thinks. *I haven't made any real effort to integrate the whole time I've been on board, I'm solitary and sullen and I keep my big ideas to myself. Well, Liam excepted.* She's conscious that she needs to respond. 'It's good of you to say so,' she mumbles at length, not sure what her face is betraying right now. Wondering why she can't manage a more convincing simulation of gratitude; not at Bao's intrusion, but at the unearned compliment.

'It's the truth,' replies Bao.

'But if this report is the basis for assessing my project's continuance… I don't have anything.' Just footage of distant zeps, with speculative annotations on their behaviour. Nothing solid.

'Then you need to find something, and write it up,' urges Bao. 'Within the next five daycycles. It need not be anything especially substantial. Everyone understands that zep communication is not a straightforward field of study—at least, anyone who knows anything about Rousseau. But there will be an expectation of some significant identifiable increment of progress.'

'Such as?'

'I don't know the field,' they answer. 'You will be better placed to assess that than anyone. Just… try to find something.' For a few seconds it's as though a mask has fallen. 'What she's trying to do to you is not fair, in any sense.' They turn towards the door, evidently having delivered what they intended to.

Well, she thinks, when the door seals following Bao's departure. *Tangible progress, and a writeup of tangible progress, within the next five daycycles, or I'm off the* Stranger. *No pressure, then.*

She sniffs the air and shrugs.

The migraine's back, with renewed vigour.

Daycycle 68, later / WS-358.45R

It's not clear, yet, whether Rousseauvian biology is any less clear-cut than Earth's, or whether it's just that the discipline is a young one. It is fair to say, at least, that the breadth and variety of its lifeforms is, at least, not less strange than Earth's. Rousseau sustains creatures which are animal, which are plant, which are both and neither, which are one thing masquerading as the other. Sanna has told Solveig of a night-blooming plantform that explodes on first contact with the rays of Rousseau's sun; Rewi has described a widely-distributed airborne chemotroph that feeds by releasing and then slowly consuming a mist of nonviable but photochemically active spores which harvest the hydrocarbons permeating the planet's atmosphere. There are other chemotrophs so specialised that their 'male' and 'female' forms are best distinguished by their ability to metabolise only one or the other enantiomer of an optically active branched-chain alkene excreted as a waste product by certain aerofauna; there are plants that hunt animals; there are creatures like the doily that will attempt to absorb, and consume, anything with which they come into contact, even themselves. Against this backdrop, Torsten's revelation of some unexpected and as yet only loosely-explored familial connection between zep and remora falls perhaps somewhat short of revolutionary.

Though it will, of course, suffice to secure Golden Boy's position within the onboard research complement for the foreseeable future.

Solveig's not sure where her bitterness arises from. Perhaps it's the knowledge that while Torsten's discovery is secure in its biochemical footing, her elucidation—of what she believes to be close common ancestry for remora and taniwha—rests, at this stage, on nothing more tangibly useful than guesswork and conviction. It's not much on which to be building a case for continuance. But what else does she have? Verifiable demonstration of a comprehension of zep communication modes? Hardly. Demonstration, even, of zep willingness to engage in the attempt of communication with humans? No. All she has is a copious bank of moderate-quality recording of zep behaviour that is, for the most part, as mundane as it is resistant to reliable interpretation. It adds significantly to the body of data they have on zeps, but that's all. It's not enough.

It is especially not enough because it has only come about through her usurpation of the *Wayfaring Stranger*'s flight plan for the purposes of one set of observations, from which she cannot realistically hope to produce anything substantive enough to cement her place once the zeps have dispersed, and once the airship has moved on to recoup opportunities lost elsewhere. She might as well have consumed a month of irreplaceable telescope time to stare at a patch of utterly-dead sky.

She needs a breakthrough, and she has none. Nor any real prospect of securing one within the next R-day or so.

She needs to try something audacious. And she does not want to contemplate the one seriously audacious act that occurs to her.

On the bright side, though, those from whom she'd need to seek permission will never green-light it, so where is the risk in asking?

The risk is that she doesn't know if it's a good decision.

Tomorrow. She will sleep on it, and by tomorrow she will have decided whether this is seriously something to pursue, no matter the likelihood of securing approval.

nine

(Safe occupancy limit: one crewmember, with parachute)

Daycycle 73, shift 1 / WS-359.34R

There's a redolent chill to the air in the auxiliary lock, a scent of perfumed bleach that seems to adhere to every surface, a tactile thrum propagating through the lock's plated flooring. All of these aspects, the entirety of the auxiliary lock, her skysuit itself—an unfamiliar space within an unfamiliar space—contribute to her sense of clumsiness. By way of contrast, Liam appears almost perfectly unencumbered by his suit. Which means he's tending to most of the tasks that she needs to be heeding for herself.

He helps her with her own suit, instructing her on the mechanisms by which it communicates with and safeguards its occupant. She's no stranger to suits, but this is different enough to a groundsuit that it leaves her feeling inexperienced, ill-informed. And sore around the wrists; something's pressing uncomfortably against her flesh there, every time she moves an arm.

'This is a really bad idea, Doc,' he says, while he checks the fastenings on her harness for what must be the fifth time. Sixth, perhaps.

'You're the third person to have told me that,' she replies, unable to keep all trace of nerves out of her voice. They're standing in the *Wayfaring Stranger*'s auxiliary lock (which like pretty much all airlocks everywhere is cramped, clad in the kind of off-white that's supposed to look reassuring but isn't, and liberally decorated with the small, official species of warning labels that a person in a mindset of unease just could not parse if her life depended on it). It doesn't help, of course, that the airlock's location at the gondola's nadir ensures an exaggerated susceptibility to every sashay and dip, every swerve of wind-induced motion, in a small space lacking exterior viewports. It also doesn't help that much of the 'floor' is the outer lock itself, a recessed (and presumably robust) plate which will slide away to reveal the deep-descending sky beneath, nor that much of the remaining floor surface has necessarily been requisitioned by the industrial-looking winch and spool assembly which has been anchored to it. There's an ominously narrow strip of flooring—a ledge, really, not more—on the port side, where they are both currently standing, and a similar ledge, soon to become inaccessible, on the starboard. It's a space which is demonstrably ill-suited to the use Solveig is seeking to put it to, but there are no alternative venues for this venture.

'So, me, yourself … who was the third?' he asks.

'Okay, fourth person,' says Solveig. 'If you want to be like that. But no, I was meaning Hong and Captain Gill. Technically, it's an EVA, so I needed to get authorisation, both from the head of Science and from the Captain. I may have muddied the waters a little.'

'How d'you mean?'

'I gave each of them to understand that I'd cleared it with the other first.'

'That's running a risk. If they ever talk—'

'I'm full of them, today.' She pauses, weighs her helmet in her hand. 'What did you say the breaking strain on the cable was?'

'It's eight-thirty kay gee. And there's a full two hundred metres of it on the spool, which is plenty. And the spool is clamped to the stanchions on the lock floor with four-tonne-secure band clamps, and the winch to drive the spool is—'

'Alright, I don't need the full rundown on the equipment. I *trust* you when you say it's not going to break.'

'Damn right it's not going to break. Just the same, you do know how to work your chute, don't you?'

'If it's not going to break, why do I need to know how to open the chute?'

'Just humour me, Doc.'

It's harder than she imagined. Much, much harder.

She's made her peace with the idea of the winched descent, the linguist-on-a-rope; she's not utterly comfortable with the concept of dangling fifteen, sixteen-odd kilometres above whatever unyielding geological feature they happen to be traversing right this moment, but she's willing to accept it as necessity. (And it is, after all, entirely her idea, which from the warm comfort of her bed this morning, just a few brief hours ago, seemed such an astoundingly *good* idea …) The letting go, though? No, she's not prepared for that at all, is almost ashamed to admit, even to herself, that she'd completely elided that necessary part of the procedure in her envisaging of the operation.

Liam sees her distress, her hesitancy. 'It's like the cold-water pool on Drum Two,' he suggests. 'Best way is just to step off, get it over with.'

'Liam,' she says, straining to make earnest eye contact through their helmets' not particularly clean faceplates, 'I *can't*.'

'You want to abort?'

She casts her mind back to the dream, to the impossible vision of 'touching down' on a zep. She sucks in a mouthful of cold, canned air, breathes out audibly between her teeth. 'No,' she says, 'I don't want to abort. But I can't just step out of the lock. I just can't.'

'Okay, then your best bet is going to be climbing off. Doing a slow-motion abseil.'

'Liam, I don't think I can do that either.'

'Why not?'

'I just—'

'Doc—Solveig—if you genuinely want to do this thing, I know you can manage it. Even if you're telling yourself it's impossible. I can help.'

'I know you can help. You'll be operating the winch, and I'm very grateful—'

'No, I mean I can help you climb down. If you get on your hands and knees, and back out of the airlock, I'll help take your weight until you're ready to let go.'

'Liam, we're fifteen or sixteen klicks up. *You're not wearing a parachute.*'

'I'll keep a firm hold of the winch at the same time. Don't worry, Doc, I have no intention of going out that lock.'

'Mice and men.'

'Huh?'

'Never mind. Look, I suppose we could try it, but why does it have to be hands and knees? Why don't I just lie prone and slide myself out?'

'It's best to avoid friction on the harness. Not that it should cause any problems, but it's always best not to take chances.'

'Says the man without a parachute. Okay, where do you want me to kneel?'

The stated purpose of the EVA is probe retrieval: FW1's reserves of buoyancy gas have been utterly consumed. The probe, which it's estimated will in ten minutes drift to a point one hundred and seventy metres directly beneath the gondola, isn't capable of a remotely instructed return to the *Wayfaring Stranger*, nor of the directionality required for data transmission to her base station, and Solveig is hungry for its stored data. For this purpose, she has a lightweight cargo net in a housing at her suit's hip; but she's hoping that this is not all the EVA is about.

Liam has called her. She doesn't respond straightaway. Sensory overload, perhaps. But it's impossible to forget the ever-present danger for more than an instant … She takes in her surroundings again, tries to read the environment rather than merely sightsee. Above, and still dominant in the sky, though it no longer shades her, is the *Wayfaring Stranger*. Around her, at varying distances (mostly of several kilometres), there are zeps at ENE, elevation +06 degrees (Lirit); NNE, elevation -02 degrees

(Colwyn); NW, elevation +02 degrees (Gajendra); W, elevation +03 degrees (Harper); SSW, elevation -01 degrees (Berit); and ESE, elevation -68 degrees (Jauhera). It is this sixth zep which has compelled Solveig to indulge in risk-taking behaviour, because in fifteen to twenty minutes' time, assuming Jauhera does not alter her course, she will pass almost directly underneath the *Wayfaring Stranger*, at a separation of less than three hundred metres.

Solveig, suspended from a cable that, at maximum extension, is two hundred metres long, will be substantially closer to the zep than to the airship. If she dares.

'Doc?' Liam prompts.

'Sorry,' she replies. 'Still here … I'm not sure how it's going to go. Won't know until I've tried. They're not cooperative like the taniwha. How far out have you played the cable?'

'About forty metres.'

'There's another forty to go? Out of two hundred?'

'No, there's another one hundred and sixty to go, out of two hundred. If you want it.'

'Are you sure?'

'About the measurement? Sure I'm sure.'

'But that means … that zep below me is twice as far as I thought it was.'

'Haven't you been using the helmet's rangefinding?'

'You didn't show me rangefinding! You just showed me directional! And if it's twice as far, that makes it … Liam, zeps are *huge*.'

'I believe other researchers may have already beaten you to that one. Are you going to want me to lower you further? Okay either way. This is your bright idea, after all.'

'Yes, lower. Might as well be hung for a goose as a lamb.'

The sky, of course, is not just zeps. As she descends, she watches as a dangler, blown in like some Portuguese man-o-war of the air, succeeds in trailing just one deadly, highly-adhesive tentacle across the envelope of a half-grown bloon. There's a kind of dreadful beauty, a butcher's skill, in the gentle, practised, delicate manner in which the dangler moves its bulk in on its kill, and then starts the process of feeding. ('It can take several hours,' Rewi has told her. 'The tricky thing is that the predator doesn't necessarily always have room for that additional buoyancy gas—the extra hydrogen, I mean. So it may need to distend one or more of its reservoir bladders, or even to grow a new one, and that can take time.')

On this occasion, the dangler doesn't have time. Solveig scarcely sees the ribbonwing before it flashes across her field of view, its razor-sharp wing slashing the dangler's envelope. The dangler, ruptured and losing buoyancy gas, starts to descend, fastening further tentacles onto the bloon on which it now depends for any remaining buoyancy. Solveig watches in fascination as the doomed creature—for the ribbonwing is plainly not going to leave off now—matches pace with her own descent, looking like some grotesque parody of a hot-air balloon, until another pass from the ribbonwing rips the badly-ruptured dangler, spraying precious fluids in a gas-strewn cascade, more-or-less free of any purchase on the still-buoyant bloon.

Solveig turns towards—

There's a tug on the cable by which she's suspended, and Liam's normally-calming tenor blooms in her earpiece. 'Doc,' he says, 'zep's rising. We need to get you up and inside.' And with that the winched cable pauses, then pulls upwards. She's being hauled in.

'Liam!' she protests, trying futilely to turn around. She can't even see the zep from here, and all her motion has achieved is to set her swaying awkwardly from the cable's anchorage. *If I knew how to work the attitude controls on this suit…*

'Collision course,' he explains. 'I'm boosting the revs on this thing. Hang on.'

Hang on? To what? Something about the cable's more frantic pull induces a slight spin, and the zep slides into view, a looming planet beneath her. It is indeed rising appreciably, faster even than she is, though she's still having problems with the scale of the creature below…

The cable, the suit. The huge sky. The zep, which up this close is a horizon all its own. She suddenly realises how truly small a creature she is.

The cable stops its ascent. She's just hanging suspended, a slow, wobbling pendulum, while beneath her the zep pushes upwards. Closer. The zep's ascent, brutally purposeful—it must have defecated hundreds of litres of ballast to be suddenly rising so fast—does not speak of anything so innocent as simple curiosity. '*Liam*—'

'Sorry,' he says. 'I just had to— it'll go faster now.' And the sudden yank of the cable at her back knocks her breathless. She's being tugged upwards uncomfortably fast.

They're in the airlock, the outer lock not yet closed, when Jauhera collides with the *Wayfaring Stranger*'s envelope. The gondola is canted sharply, Solveig—still tethered to the winch cable—is slammed into the airlock's unyielding side wall. When she picks herself up, the gondola swaying drunkenly, Liam's not there.

He's not there. The outer lock's open. Sixteen kilometres. He's not wearing a parachute.

She feels sick, faint, dizzy, deafened, none of which she has time for. With shaking, glove-impeded fingers reaching blindly behind her, she struggles with the cable's anchorage with her suit, finds the release after too many seconds. Turns to the inner lock, through which, beckoning, she can see a second parachute, wall-mounted and waiting.

Time. Time is what she does not have.

She takes a second, two, three, profligate, to check that her own parachute's securely tethered to her suit, then she turns toward the outer lock. Steps around the winch housing.

And jumps.

ten

Daycycle 73, shift 1 / WS-359.34R

She can't see him. She's got the busy air, with its bubbleheads, its bloons, its grapefloats streaming blurringly past her as she falls, buffeted and pushed by the air's resistive bulk; there are skeins of smoky cirrus, sentinels of the haze deck, growing slowly larger as she nears them; zeps toward the horizon in several directions; and, looking up, squinting against the still-bright glare of the sun, she sees silhouetted the *Wayfaring Stranger* and, she presumes, the zep which rammed it (and which, so far as she can tell, is moving off, its message delivered). But Liam? No.

She's trying to remember how many seconds she lost, how many hundreds of metres' head start he must have on her. She *has* to find him. She has to somehow catch him: another small human in a big, big sky. Falling towards—

For moments she believes the task utterly hopeless, the doom-dark ground rushing up with irresistible speed already; but it's not the ground she can see, but the lumped, insubstantial moraine of the haze deck. The despair is palpable, difficult to breathe through. Then she marshals herself, and has the suit find his channel. More seconds wasted.

'Liam?' Her own voice, echoed within the skysuit's helmet, sounds ragged, scraped raw, distorted by the roar of Rousseau's air past the protective carapace of her suit. There's no response. 'Liam?'

It's just a crackle; then it resolves itself, on repetition, into a word. 'Doc?'

'Solveig,' she corrects him, then wishes she hadn't. 'Inbound. Can't see you. Light up.'

And then she sees him, before he's had time to activate his lamps, as he slams spread-eagled through a carpetform. She quickly zooms her helmet's display: for a couple of juddering seconds there's a cartoonish person-shaped breach in the carpet's surface, tugged this way and that as she tries to hold her head still; then the carpetform convulses, crumples, and starts to fall towards the haze-deck. She's lost Liam again, but at least now she has a heading. And the impact presumably will have slowed his descent, if only fractionally. If he stays prone, while she head-dives, then maybe … 'Liam?' she calls again.

She sees him before he answers, his suit's lamps slight but bright against the looming dark of the haze deck. He's three hundred metres below her, almost as many away in horizontal displacement. It's the latter which terrifies her: the vertical gap she can perhaps close, if sufficient altitude remains, but how to close the lateral gulf? She can't see a way.

Then the darkness takes him.

She views the up-rushing blanket of haze with concern, maybe fear. It's not just the limited visibility; the haze hides things. There are few better places to look for aerial ambush predators.

Too late; it's around her.

From within, the haze is murky, but not monolithically opaque. It takes on a skeined character, striped by shade and phosphorescence alike: the lighting's too dim, too uncertain for her to distinguish any more definite features. But she knows—

There's a thump, so violent that for a second she believes it to be that final impact, the intersection of Solveig with the unremitting surface of the planet. But it's only a mantawing, a juvenile of, she thinks, barely two metres' length, spied fleetingly and indistinctly as a leather-winged shape of deeper darkness as she caroms off it, falls past. A few more seconds while, heart thudding, she waits to learn if the casing of her suit is intact.

She blacks out with the force of the second impact, six seconds after the first.

She comes to with her left leg a map of agony and with the taste of blood sharp and full-bodied in her mouth. Gravity's tug on her is at full strength: she's no longer falling. She's lying more-or-less on her side in a deep, close darkness and, quite aside from the hideous pain of her leg, she's pretty sure she hurts all over.

The ground shakes, twists, gradually pulls her upward a short distance. (*Upward?*)

She's not dead. Not yet, at any rate. Which means that, whatever it is she has slammed into, it's not the unforgiving tar-grit regolith surface of Rousseau. She tries to move. Shrieks. The ground shakes again.

'Doc?'

The voice in her helmet is rasped, anguished, fills her with torment. She can't ever intercept his fall now. All she can manage is to listen, to witness the final few seconds of Liam Subramanian's existence, as he plummets towards that killing impact. She owes him that, it's on her account that he's fallen to his death, but she can't; she just can't.

She mutes the audio. Hating herself, accusing herself of disloyalty; but she doesn't have the strength to do otherwise. She is trying once again to pull herself free when there's a thud behind her, followed shortly after by a juddering wobble to the surface beneath her. It knocks her down, sends fresh jolts of pain through her leg. But now she knows where she is; or at least, what it is she has landed on.

A doily; and clearly a big one. Forty metres in width, at least.

It's likely the collision with the mantawing saved her life, by spinning her more-or-less upright and averting a helmet-first fall against the non-Newtonian net of the doily. But Liam's gone, and it's her fault.

It's difficult to breathe.

Seconds have passed, possibly minutes. She tries to ignore the diminishing tremors that pulse through the surface beneath her while, she presumes, the doomed mantawing struggles to escape the doily's toxic hold on it.

How long does it take to fall eight kilometres, at terminal velocity? How long does he have?

There's still an incoming call. On the private channel.

She unmutes.

'Doc?'

She will not cry. She just won't. 'Liam?'

'Doc,' he replies, and the relief in his voice is both palpable and, for her, incriminatory. 'I'm *stuck.*'

Then she realises what those words must mean. This will shame her, for however long she has left to live, that she left him muted while he lay damaged and without means of escape, on the same huge doily on which she has impacted.

For now, though, her task is this: to find him and, somehow, to reach him. Movement hurts, and the doily's corrosively adhesive surface encourages immobility, but she must do this. And she needs to do it before the doily's metabolism registers that there are no nutrients to usefully acquire from this windfall.

'Liam?' she asks again. 'Light up, please.'

He does so, and her spirit sags. The glow is faint and distant. *One hundred and seventy-three metres*, her helmet assures her.

'Can you move?' she asks.

'I'm stuck,' is all he can say, and he may well have too many points of contact with the doily to detach any of them.

She's more fortunate in that regard. She pulls an arm free from the doily's cloying embrace, stretches it forward, grabs an adjacent cable of the thick black sticky lacework that gives the doily its name. Pulls herself bodily Liamwards, not caring that the doily is bunching behind her. Whatever it takes. A fresh burst of complaint from her seemingly shattered leg.

One hundred and seventy-two metres, the helmet advises.

Whatever it takes.

*

She rests briefly, grits her teeth against the incessant signals of pain from her shin. Behind her, the mantawing's efforts have seemingly ceased; hers must not. She requests the suit's aid with pain management, something she has been delaying as long as possible.

One hundred and twenty-five metres.

She extends her free arm forward once more. Whatever it takes.

An epiphany, unwanted for now: the doily is, in form though not at all in function, an analogy in some sense to the zep's attitude sinus, a network or web, approximately circular in one instance, prolately spheroidal in the other, through which fluids—a froth of buoyancy gas and digestive juices for the doily, ballast liquid for the zep—are shepherded to achieve a useful outcome for the organism. Are they perhaps connected? Is this a further piece of possible evidence for a haze-deck origin for the zep's ancestors, as for the remoras and the taniwha? Are the doilies in some sense ancestral to all those forms? There's no way of knowing, might never be.

One hundred and four metres.

The doily's grip appears less tenacious now, as though it is learning that this strange stubborn prey item is not worth the effort. Or perhaps it is focussed upon feeding on the enmeshed mantawing. It's difficult to concentrate, though, with the strong analgesia with which the suit has clouded her.

It ends with this: she reaches him, where he lies ten metres from the doily's frayed edge. He is indeed stuck fast; but she extricates him, limb by limb, helmet, torso, drags him towards that edge. They are perhaps five metres from the doily's perimeter when it decides it has had enough of their indigestible freeloading; it flexes so they fall free.

She grabs hold: whatever happens, she will not now let him go. Not until this is done.

They fall together, through the remainder of the haze-deck, then through the dusklight of Rousseau's lower atmosphere, past the montgolfiers and the mantawings towards the planet's unforgiving surface. She must keep hold of him, it's important that her arms pass under his, lock tightly around his suit, which means she can't operate the release on the parachute; he needs to twist in her embrace to achieve this.

The chute emerges. She strengthens her grip. Then it's a matter of waiting those few seconds as it deploys, this one-person chute she is hoping will bear a two-person load.

acknowledgments

If you found this book readable, this is in large part due to the general excellence of James Morrison's editing. Thanks are also due to James for supplying an eye-catching cover visualisation of my imagined world. Kudos, too, to Octavia Cade, Adam Browne and Thoraiya Dyer for allowing their kind words to appear on the cover; I am further indebted (though not, I should clarify, in any financial capacity) to family and friends for putting up with my nonsense as a writer.

Finally, of course, any errors, imperfections, etc. in the story are my own work, for which I accept full responsibility.

about the author

Born and raised in North Canterbury, New Zealand, Simon Petrie now lives in Canberra, Australia, where he is paid to be careful with words. He has been shortlisted several times for the Sir Julius Vogel, Ditmar, and Aurealis Awards, and has won the Sir Julius Vogel Award three times: in 2010 for Best New Talent and in 2013 and 2018, with *Flight 404* and *Matters Arising from the Identification of the Body* respectively, for Best Novella. He also scored a coveted Dishonourable Mention in the 2011 Bulwer-Lytton Fiction Contest.

He has edited five issues (numbers 35, 40, 51, 54, and 61) of *Andromeda Spaceways Inflight Magazine*, and has co-edited two anthologies (*Light Touch Paper, Stand Clear* and *Use Only As Directed*) with Edwina Harvey and one (*Next*) with Rob Porteous.

A reformed academic, Simon's publishing history also includes numerous studies on the upper-atmosphere chemistry of the Saturnian moon Titan; on the ion/molecule chemistry of the dense interstellar cloud TMC-1 and the circumstellar envelope of the post-asymptotic-giant-branch star IRC+10216; on the gas-phase chemistry of multiply-charged fullerene ions; and on the structure of the active site of the water-oxidising complex within Photosystem II. He holds actionable views about second person present tense, em-dashes, and Oxford commas.

also by this author

Wide Brown Land (stories of Titan)
A collection of eleven hard-SF short stories set on the Solar System's most intriguing moon.
Paperback: 978-0-6483228-2-5
Ebook: 978-0-6483228-3-2

Soft Dim Skies
It's important to Cory that his past misdeeds aren't uncovered. It's important to Portia that her mentor's death hasn't been in vain. A novella, connecting several threads begun in *Wide Brown Land*.
Paperback: 978-0-6483836-5-9
Ebook: 978-0-6483836-6-6

Matters Arising From The Identification Of The Body
Tanja Morgenstein, daughter of a wealthy industrialist and a geochemist, is dead from exposure to Titan's lethal, chilled atmosphere, and Guerline Scarfe must determine why.
(Winner of the 2018 Sir Julius Vogel award for Best Novella.)
Paperback: 978-0-6483228-0-1
Ebook: 978-0-6483228-1-8

Flight 404
The search for the Bougainvillaea brings investigator Charmaine Mertz back to the unwelcoming world of her boyhood.
(Winner of the 2013 Sir Julius Vogel award for Best Novella.)
Paperback: 978-0-6483228-4-9
Ebook: 978-0-6483228-5-6

The 1001 Top Immortality Treatments You Must Try Before You Die
Short fiction, including: the poignant tale of the world's first sentient academic journal; a daring rescue attempt on the searing surface of Venus; the details now known about Apollo 15's secret fourth astronaut; and a mercifully-short poem written entirely in Webdings.
Paperback: 978-0-6483836-3-5
Ebook: 978-0-6483836-4-2

80,000 Totally Secure Passwords That No Hacker Would Ever Guess
If a collection of unconnected short stories can have (or be) a companion volume, then this is the companion volume to *The 1001 Top Immortality Treatments You Must Try Before You Die.*
Paperback: 978-0-6483228-6-3
Ebook: 978-0-6483228-7-0

Murder On The Zenith Express (the Gordon Mamon collection)
The (now no longer quite complete) adventures of space-hotel employee and reluctant sleuth Gordon Mamon.
Paperback: 978-0-6483228-8-7
Ebook: 978-0-6483228-9-4

Tremendously Inconveniencing A Great Many Photons
An uplifting short novel about pottos, First Contact, and interstellar spaceflight.
Paperback: 978-0-6483836-1-1
Ebook: 978-0-6483836-2-8